THE Sisters 8

BOOK 1

ANNIE'S ADVENTURES

By Lauren Baratz-Logsted
With Greg Logsted & Jackie Logsted

Illustrated by Lisa K. Weber

sandpiper

HOUGHTON MIFFLIN HARCOURT

BOSTON 2008

www.houghtonmifflinbooks.com

Sandpiper and the Sandpiper logo are trademarks of the
Houghton Mifflin Harcourt Publishing Company.

The text of this book is set in Youbee.
Text design by Carol Chu.

Library of Congress Cataloging-in-Publication Data
Baratz-Logsted, Lauren.
Annie's adventures / by Lauren Baratz-Logsted ;
with Greg Logsted and Jackie Logsted.
p. cm. — (The sisters eight ; bk. 1)
Summary: On New Year's Eve, the octuplets Huit—Annie, Durinda,
Georgia, Jackie, Marcia, Petal, Rebecca, and Zinnia—discover that
their parents are missing, and then uncover a mysterious note
instructing them that each must find her power and her gift if they
want to know what happened to their parents.
ISBN 978-0-547-13349-2 (hardcover)
ISBN 978-0-547-05338-7 (paperback)
[1. Sisters—Fiction. 2. Abandoned children—Fiction.]
I. Logsted, Greg. II. Logsted, Jackie. III. Title.
PZ7.B22966An 2008
[Fic]—dc22
2008000602

Printed in the United States of America
MP 10 9 8 7 6 5 4 3 2 1

For Julia Richardson,
obviously and with love

Annie   Durinda   Georgia   Jackie

Marcia   Petal   Rebecca   Zinnia

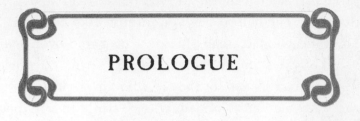

PROLOGUE

The story always begins the same.

Once upon a time, there were eight sisters who would all one day be eight years old.

At the same time.

They were octuplets, you see.

Their names were Annie, Durinda, Georgia, Jackie, Marcia, Petal, Rebecca, and Zinnia. They were each born a minute apart on August 8, 2000. All eight had brown hair and brown eyes. And although they were all the same exact age, give or take a few minutes, each was one inch taller than the next, with Zinnia being the shortest and Annie the tallest.

And their story always begins the same, so:

Please stop reading if you have read about the Sisters Eight before, and go directly to chapter one.

Please keep reading if you have not read about the Sisters Eight before.

Please keep reading if you have read about the Sisters Eight before but your memory is lousy.

Please keep reading if you have read about the Sisters Eight before but you simply like the writing here and want to read this part over and over again.

Eight girls in one story, or one series of stories. This is bad news for boys, who may suspect that there are no snails or puppy dogs' tails in this book. However, there *might* be snails and puppy dogs' tails, but the only way you will ever know this is to read further. Remember: girls can be just as grubby as boys—you just have to give them half a chance.

The family name of the Sisters Eight was Huit, which is French for *eight* and pronounced like "wheat," as in cream of, which I hope you never have to eat. On New Year's Eve 2007, as you shall soon see, their parents disappeared, or died, one of the two—this was a fine holiday present for the sisters, let me tell you.

Parents disappeared, presumed dead, actually dead—parents don't fare very well in children's stories these days, I'm afraid. Best to be a child and not a parent, then.

The Sisters Eight lived in a magnificent stone house, which you will see more of very soon. It could practically have been a castle. It was therefore not the kind of house you would want to leave under any circumstances, certainly not after your parents had disappeared. Or died. You would not want to be taken away from your sisters, separated. And so they had to endeavor—as you would no doubt do too—to hang on to their home and to one another, keeping the truth away from the prying eyes of adults, who would surely have split them all up like so many stalks of wheat cast upon the wind.

Not an easy task—sticking together with loved ones—when you are seven, soon to be eight.

And where was this magnificent stone house? Why, it might have been anywhere in the world— even right next door to you—so why quibble? However, if there were octuplets in your class at school, you would probably have noticed by now, so perhaps that's not the case.

One thing was for sure: there were undoubtedly many cats in this almost castle, cats who would also have been taken away if word got out that the parents of the Sisters Eight had disappeared. Or died.

As we approach the beginning of our first adventure, it is that fateful New Year's Eve 2007 and the girls are about to discover the disappearance of their parents— odd, the idea of discovering that which has disappeared—as well as a note hidden behind a loose stone in the wall of the drawing room of their magnificent home. The note reads:

Dear Annie, Durinda, Georgia, Jackie,
Marcia, Petal, Rebecca, and Zinnia,

This may come as rather a shock to
you, but it appears you each possess a
power and a gift. The powers you
already have—you merely don't
know you have them yet. The gifts
are from your parents, and these you
must also discover for yourselves. In
fact, you must each discover both
your power and your gift in order to
reveal what happened to your parents.
Have you got all that?

The note is unsigned.

And what *has* happened to their parents? Well, we
don't know that yet, do we? If we did, then this would
be the end of our story, not the beginning . . .

CHAPTER ONE

It was New Year's Eve 2007, approximately ten o'clock, and we were just getting ready to celebrate Christmas.

This may seem an odd time to celebrate Christmas, but on December 25, we had been stranded by snowstorms in Utah. Our parents had decreed that we celebrate our belated holiday on the eve of another holiday, and so we were about to enjoy a twofer. Or so we thought.

"But where are the presents?" asked Zinnia.

We were in the drawing room, which sounds like a room you draw pictures in but that we actually just sit in. On this night, we were sitting around a dying fire, waiting for something exciting to happen.

Betty came in with her dust cloth, which wasn't exciting at all. Betty was our mother's invention, a black and gold robot designed to make our life easier by doing the cleaning. But something had gone wrong with Betty's programming.

"Why don't you dust the floor under the tree?" Zinnia suggested to Betty. "That way, it will be cleaner there when our presents arrive."

Betty took the dust cloth, which she had draped over one of her accordion arms, and with one pincered hook placed it upon her own head.

Do you see what we mean about Betty?

"Good job, Betty," Zinnia said. Really, what else could one say?

"Bye, Betty!" we all shouted after her as she exited the room. Betty would probably now head outdoors to dust under the wrong tree.

The drawing room was our favorite room of the house. There was a grandfather clock and even a suit of armor propped in one corner. Daddy always said every home should have one—the suit of armor, not the clock. Daddy hated clocks. The walls of the room were made out of big slats of gray stone, which was cool in summer, but not so hot in winter.

"Perhaps Mommy and Daddy are waiting until we go to sleep, as usual," Annie said to Zinnia, "and why do you always have to worry so much about presents anyway?"

"I don't know why you have to be so bossy," Durinda said to Annie.

"Because she's the oldest," Georgia said. There was

something sneering about the way she said it, like she was thinking of staging a coup.

"Do you always have to sneer so much, Georgia?" said Petal in a rare stab at speaking out of turn. Petal was our shy girl.

"The mouse roars," observed Rebecca snidely.

"I don't think you should pick on Petal," said Jackie, our peacemaker.

"And I don't know why you have to stick up for everyone all the time," observed Georgia. Then she sighed. "I'm bored."

"How can you be bored?" Annie asked. "You got caught in an avalanche in Utah. Wasn't that enough excitement for you?"

Georgia yawned. "It was just a tiny avalanche. I could have swam out myself if you'd only left me there another hour."

"Excuse me," said Marcia, staring into the rapidly diminishing fire in the fireplace, "but hasn't anyone noticed something is missing?"

"Such as?" prompted Rebecca.

"Perhaps I shouldn't have said *something*," Marcia self-corrected.

"Well," said Georgia, "if you're not going to say *something*, then why did you say *anything* at all?"

"No, not that," Marcia said, growing impatient.

"What I should have said was, 'Hasn't anyone noticed *someone* is missing?' Or some *ones?*"

"I'm afraid you've lost me," said Petal.

"Mommy and Daddy," Marcia prompted. Marcia was the observant one among us. "You know, those adults we live with?"

We looked around and realized she was right.

When had we last seen Mommy and Daddy?

Turn the clock back about twenty minutes:

"I'm going to the woodshed for logs for the fire," Daddy had said.

"I'm going to go fix a tray of eggnog for us all," Mommy had said.

"How long do you suppose," Petal asked now, "it takes a person to gather wood for a fire? Or pour ten glasses of eggnog?"

"Dunno," Zinnia said. "I suspect five minutes for the first, perhaps another three for the second if you put the carton back in the fridge. So, five and three—eight. It should have taken them eight minutes."

"But they were doing it *simultaneously,*" Georgia said, "not one after another, so they both should have been back within five minutes, tops, even if Mommy took a really long time putting the carton back. Even if she decided to bring us cookies too."

"I could be wrong," said Annie, "but I think it's a little early to file a missing-persons report."

"But they should have been back at least fifteen min-utes ago!" Zinnia said, clearly starting to panic. "More, if you consider the time we've spent talking since we realized it was twenty minutes since they disappeared!"

"Well," Annie corrected, "that's not technically true. We noticed—"

"*I* noticed," Marcia briefly cut in.

"—at the twenty-minute mark," Annie went on. "But that doesn't mean that's when they disappeared. It merely means that's when we noticed—"

"*I* noticed."

"—they weren't exactly here anymore."

"This is no time for petty squabbles about time," said Jackie. "What do you think we should *do?*"

"We should look for them, of course," Annie said. "There's no doubt some simple explanation, and when we find it, Georgia can go back to being bored and Zinnia can go back to worrying about presents."

"Okay," said Durinda. "Where should we start?"

"The kitchen?" Annie asked as much as answered.

This seemed sensible to us, mostly because going to look in the kitchen was a lot less scary than going out into the dark night to look for Daddy in the woodshed.

So we rose as one. Even though it seemed a safe thing to do—go to the kitchen to look for our parents—

we walked with caution, as if we might find an ax murderer there. In fact, before leaving the drawing room entirely, Annie grabbed the silver spear from the suit of armor's grasp.

"Insurance," she whispered.

"Mommy!" we all called softly as we tiptoed. "Daddy!" we called, in case he'd snuck in the back door.

In the kitchen, where we all ate breakfast together in the mornings before school, there was the usual boring kitchen stuff. There were the sharp knives, all still thankfully in their blocks; we checked. There was the tile floor that was so much fun to skate across, and the big picture window that looked out over the hill. There was even the talking refrigerator Mommy had invented. But there was no Mommy, no Daddy.

Immediately, Annie crossed to the fridge. She opened the door slowly.

"Fully stocked larder," the talking refrigerator said. "No need to shop." The refrigerator was always saying things that didn't matter to us, since we didn't have to do the shopping. It was always encouraging us to eat more too. The refrigerator thought we were too skinny.

We ignored the talking refrigerator as Annie pulled out a half-gallon carton and held it up for all to see. In big, cheery red and green letters, the carton read *Eggnog* on the front.

"It hasn't even been opened," Annie said.

"Then where did Mommy go before?" Rebecca asked. "And where's Daddy? And what do we do now?" Fear had replaced her testiness.

"We search the rest of the house, of course," Annie said.

And so we did.

We moved through the house: the bedrooms, six bathrooms, closets, the tower room, the seasonal rooms—we won't talk about the seasonal rooms right now, but we did go through them. We even checked the basement, although Petal didn't want to on account of the spiders.

Still no parents.

Last, we checked Mommy's study, but only briefly poking our heads in. It was a room we were normally forbidden to enter.

"What now, Sherlock?" Georgia addressed Annie.

"We check out the woodshed, of course," Annie said.

And, suddenly, fear was back for everybody.

It is one thing to look for your parents inside a house when you fully expect to find them somewhere, but it is quite another to venture outside when you are pretty sure both your parents have mysteriously disappeared.

Still, what else were we to do?

"I'll get everyone's coats," Durinda offered, "boots too."

"I'll get the knives," Jackie said, "for everyone."

"But aren't you supposed to be our pacifist?" Marcia observed.

"I've got my spear," Annie said, ignoring Marcia.

Outside, it was easy enough to follow in Daddy's footsteps; we were guided between the trees by the light from the moon. The footsteps went in one direction—toward the shed—with no return.

Carefully, we placed our booted steps in the holes he'd left in the snow.

"I'll go in first," Annie announced as we neared the woodshed. This was a very brave thing to do—also good timing, since none of the rest of us were feeling that brave right then. And, you know, she had the spear.

Annie threw the door open hard, like a cop on a TV program who's about to make a bust. It was such a bold move. We were proud of her.

Bravery, boldness—all for nothing. Daddy wasn't in the woodshed any more than Mommy had been in the kitchen. Wherever our parents were, wherever they had disappeared to at approximately ten o'clock in the night on New Year's Eve, they weren't in the woodshed.

Back to the house we trudged, through our father's steps, cold and dejected now. Worried too.

We removed our coats and boots and laid down our weapons. Except for Annie. She was enjoying holding that silver spear an awful lot.

"What do we do now?" Petal asked, rather petulantly we thought. "What's happened to Mommy and Daddy?"

"They've disappeared, obviously," Georgia said.

"Or else they're dead," Rebecca put in.

"Stop frightening Petal and Zinnia," Jackie said evenly.

"Well, aren't *you* frightened?" Georgia demanded.

Jackie tilted her head to one side and considered this. "Yes and no," she finally said. "I think we should have some eggnog and think."

"You get the eggnog," Annie instructed Durinda and Jackie, "while I stoke the fire." At that last, she removed a log she'd hidden in her coat while we were all out at the woodshed. She'd taken it without us noticing—we were that worried about Mommy and Daddy—although we had noticed she looked rather larger. And we were thankful of course that she'd thought to bring the log. The fire was nearly dead.

Once we were all gathered back in the drawing room, the fire nicely stoked, our eggnogs finally in hand, it was time to worry again.

"What do you think happened to them?" Petal asked.

"Maybe it's all a surprise," Zinnia said excitedly. "Maybe all this time they've been getting our presents, arranging them on a flying sleigh or something, and any moment now they're going to land on the roof, and—"

"I think they've just disappeared," Georgia said flatly.

"Or else they're dead," Rebecca put in.

"I wish you would all stop—" Jackie started to say, but she never got a chance to finish because right then Marcia screamed.

"That stone on the wall!"

"What?" Durinda asked, concerned, acting just like Mommy would.

Marcia pointed. "That stone in the wall! It wasn't

like that when we were in the room before! It's never been like that! It's sticking out!"

We all thought that Marcia had gone crazy from all the stress. But Durinda, still acting like Mommy, followed the direction of Marcia's finger to the offending stone. Where Durinda looked, we all looked, and that's when we saw: one of the stones *had* been disturbed!

Annie made her cautious way over to it, spear in hand. We all followed close behind her. We may have been scared but we were curious too.

Annie pried the stone the rest of the way out, revealing a secret hiding spot none of us had known about before. And in the hiding spot was the note that would change our lives. You may have seen this note already—in fact, we're sure you have—but it was a pretty important event in our lives and we hope you won't mind if we reprint it here and now:

Dear Annie, Durinda, Georgia, Jackie, Marcia, Petal, Rebecca, and Zinnia,

This may come as rather a shock to you, but it appears you each possess a power and a gift. The powers you already have—you merely don't know you have them yet. The gifts

are from your parents, and these you
must also discover for yourselves. In
fact, you must each discover both
your power and your gift in order to
reveal what happened to your parents.
Have you got all that?

The note was unsigned.

"See?" said Zinnia. "It says *gifts*. I *knew* there would
be presents!"

"I don't think this means those kinds of gifts," Annie
said.

"What do you make of this?" Durinda asked.

"It means Mommy and Daddy really have disappeared," Georgia said.

"Or else they're dead," Rebecca put in.

One tear swam out of Petal's left eye as another ran
out of Zinnia's right eye, and Jackie put her arms
around both.

Then eight sets of very similar brown eyes looked
at one another, wondering what we should do next.

As the grandfather clock struck midnight, marking
the New Year and turning us all over into 2008, Annie
turned to Georgia and spoke.

"You said you were bored. Well"—she nodded—
"I suppose we've all got plenty of excitement now."

CHAPTER TWO

"So what do we do now?" Georgia demanded.

"We feed the cats and go to bed," Annie said.

"Is that *all*?"

"Well, the cats do need to be fed."

There were eight cats living in the house, one for each of us: Anthrax, Dandruff, Greatorex, Jaguar, Minx, Precious, Rambunctious, and Zither. Each was gray and white, and it was always hard for anyone other than us to tell them apart. The cats could, of course, tell all of us apart too.

"But aren't we going to *do* anything?" Georgia insisted. "You know, about Mommy and Daddy disappearing?"

"The best thing we can do right now is take care of the cats and take care of ourselves. In the light of day, we'll see things more clearly."

And we'd have been able to see things a lot more clearly even then if the lights hadn't gone out right after we finished feeding the cats in the cat room. The cat room was like our drawing room, only for cats.

"Oh no!" Zinnia cried out. "Whatever bad person took Mommy and Daddy turned out the power—something awful is about to happen!"

"Now, now," Durinda soothed. "Annie," she directed, "call the electric company and find out what's going on. It's what Daddy would do."

So Annie stumbled her way back to the drawing room, where, with the light from the fire, she could still make out the phone.

Annie phoned Information and waited to be connected to the electric company. When we heard her speak, her voice was deeper than usual.

"Hello"—she cleared her throat—"this is Robert Huit at Eight-eight-eight Middle Way, and I was wondering if you could tell me: Is it just my power that's out, or is this a citywide problem?" She paused. "Ah, yes. Jolly good. Thanks so much. You chaps do great work." And she hung up.

"Well," Georgia said, "what's going on?"

"It started snowing again"—Annie was still speaking in her faux Daddy voice and had to make herself stop—"and they say there must have been too much ice on the lines somewhere and one of them came down. They should have it fixed by morning." She forced a smile. "I don't think we'll freeze by then if we put extra blankets on."

"Thank *God*," Petal said, "that this is affecting everyone and not just us. I was sure it was the work of the ax murderer."

"May I ask you a question?" Rebecca said to Annie.

"Of course."

"Why didn't you say you were Lucy Huit? It would have been easier to impersonate Mommy, I should think."

"Huh," Annie said. "I dunno. I guess I never thought to impersonate anyone other than Daddy."

"And what," Rebecca pressed, "was all that stuff about 'jolly good' and 'you chaps'? Daddy never talks that way! You made him sound *British!*"

"Well, but he could be British, couldn't he? I mean, the electric company doesn't know where we come from."

Rebecca harrumphed. She did not find the answer satisfying.

But we were all tired by then.

It is strange. You would think that enormous amounts of fear, the kind we'd been through, would have been enough to keep us awake for weeks. But human beings are funny things, and we Sisters Eight are nothing if not human. We yawned as a group for, in the end, fear had worn us out.

Annie took down the twin candelabras from the

mantel over the fireplace and handed one to Durinda. Then the two of them lit the three candles in each from the dwindling fire that still burned.

We made our way to bed, following behind them to our rooms on the floor above. Annie and Durinda supervised as we brushed our teeth and hair, then they did their own while we waited.

Usually, we slept in two rooms separated by a single large bathroom. In one room slept the four oldest; in the other, the youngest. But not on that night. Annie was worried that Petal and Zinnia would be too worried, Rebecca would insult their worries, and Marcia, the oldest in that room, wouldn't be able to control the situation. So she made a minor switch.

"Durinda," she said, "you sleep with the three youngest and I'll take Marcia in with us."

So that's what we did. And in a way, as Annie and Durinda made the rounds from bed to bed, tucking each of us in with a kiss by the light cast from their candelabras, this minor switch

was comforting. At least someone—Annie—was taking charge.

But as you can imagine, it was all very confusing
for the cats. It took some time for Dandruff and Minx
to find the right beds to sleep at the bottom of, but
once they did, we were all out like lights.

* * * * * * * *

We awoke to the rumble of empty stomachs and the
cats grumbling for more food. We awoke to a world
filled with light.

The power had come back on.

"Rise and shine," Annie said as she bustled around
the bedrooms.

We put on our robes and brushed our teeth, feeling as though we'd hardly slept at all. Then we made
our way downstairs to the smell of . . . nothing.

On Christmas Day and New Year's Day mornings,
Mommy always made big stacks of chocolate chip
pancakes for us. This year, since we were supposed
to be celebrating both holidays at once, we'd all secret-
ly been expecting a double dose of the good stuff. But
there was to be none of that. Or at least, none of
that made by Mommy.

"How are we going to eat?" Petal asked, puzzled.

"We're going to do it ourselves, of course," Annie said.

Petal remained puzzled, as though Annie were speaking British again.

"Okay," Annie announced, "here's what we're going to do. We'll gather whatever ingredients we think go into the pancakes and do our best."

"Actually," Durinda said timidly, "I've watched Mommy closely when she's made them. I'm pretty sure I can do it if Jackie helps me."

"I can do that," Jackie said gamely.

"Good." Annie nodded. "Georgia and Rebecca, see to the cats."

"You mean feed them?" Georgia asked.

"Feed them, of course," Annie said. She paused and then added with a meaningful sniff of the air, "Also, clean the litter boxes."

"But Mommy always does that!" Rebecca objected.

"Well," Annie said, "Mommy's not here right now, is she?"

"At least we don't have to worry about the plants," Durinda put in.

It was true.

Mommy had invented a flying watering can. It moved through the house on metal runners attached to the ceiling, stopping over each plant to give it a healthy sprinkle. Unfortunately, sometimes the flying watering can malfunctioned, sprinkling the floor—which we would then have to clean up—or even sometimes sprinkling a person.

"And what are *you* going to do," Georgia demanded of Annie, "while we're doing all of *that?*"

"I'll be planning," Annie said importantly. "Durinda, Jackie, Georgia, and Rebecca are doing breakfast and cat detail, and after we eat, Marcia, Petal, Zinnia, and myself will shovel the walk so the mailperson can get through tomorrow. Petal and Zinnia can even build snowpeople as we go, to take their minds off things. And I'll get more wood for the fire."

So that's what we did, at Annie's bidding. We went off to prepare breakfast, feed cats, and clean litter boxes.

As it turned out, to all of our wonder-filled surprise, Durinda was a fantastic cook. With Jackie's help, of course.

"Yummy," Zinnia pronounced, surrounding her pancakes with maple syrup as we sat down to our Christmas/New Year's morning breakfast, fresh juice filling our glasses. We were eight at a table that usually sat ten.

It was hard to ignore those two empty chairs.

At last, Georgia spoke the words we were all thinking. Well, she spoke them because we'd put her up to it.

While Annie was off getting the wood, we'd had a little conference and elected Georgia our spokesperson. Okay, maybe she volunteered.

"Annie," Georgia said, "I've been wondering: why didn't you call the cops right away last night?" Her words sounded innocent enough, and yet there was something about her tone that smacked of accusation.

Annie looked surprised by the question, as well as the tone. "It was New Year's Eve," she said, "late, and there was lots of snow. We live at the top of a hill. Do you think they'd have been in a hurry to rush out here? You've seen cop stories on TV. If we phoned them, they'd tell us we need to wait at least twenty-four hours to file a missing-persons report."

"Then why not call them now?" Georgia prompted.

"Because twenty-four hours haven't passed." Annie speared another bite of pancake. "It hasn't even been twelve hours yet." She popped the pancake bite into her mouth.

But Georgia wouldn't let up. "Then what about tonight at exactly ten, when it's been twenty-four hours—will you call then?"

"No," Annie said simply.

"But why ever not?" Jackie put in. Even our peacekeeper couldn't help but be confused by Annie's behavior.

"Because," Annie said evenly, "they couldn't *do* anything. And whatever they *might* do would only make a muddle of things."

"I don't think any of us follow you," Marcia said.

"Okay, then, it's like this," Annie said, setting down her fork. "We don't know what happened to Mommy and Daddy, correct?"

Seven heads nodded.

"But we did get that note," Annie went on. "Someone left it there. It's not a ransom note. It's not a threatening note. But it does tell us what to do if we want to find out what happened to our parents: we must discover our own powers and our own gifts. And that's what I propose we do."

"But how will we do *that?*" Rebecca said. "And why can't the police be looking for Mommy and Daddy while we're . . . ?" Rebecca's eyes filled with horror. "Oh no! The reason you're not calling them is that you're certain Mommy and Daddy are . . . dead!"

"Don't be daft," Annie said crossly. "Here's the situation: our mother disappeared from a kitchen where she went to make eggnog, our father disappeared from a woodshed. Now, we know our parents better than anyone in the world. On the other hand, the cops know nothing of our parents. Do you really think they can do better than we can?"

It made sense to us.

"And there's another thing," Annie said.

"Which is?" Georgia prompted.

"If we tell the cops, they'll split us up. Then, not only will we not have parents, we won't even have each other anymore."

"How do you *know* that?" Georgia asked.

"Simple logic," Annie said. "If we call the cops, they certainly won't let us go on living here without a grownup. First they'll call our relatives."

We thought about our relatives: grandparents on different continents; Aunt Martha, who'd never had children; Uncle George, who'd never liked children. And when we saw them, all of them said we were too loud.

"None of them will take all of us," Annie went on. "They might not even take *any* of us. And what do you think the chances are that they'll find a foster home that will take on eight kids at once?"

It was a question with an obvious negative answer.

"Right," Annie said. "If we call the cops, we'd be split up by nightfall."

"And how long would that go on?" Petal asked, clearly worried.

"Forever," Annie said, "if they don't find Mommy and Daddy."

Jackie was thinking. "So, then, we have to pretend everything's fine here, that there are adults still living in the house, until we can figure out what happened to Mommy and Daddy?"

"Exactly," Annie said.

We could all see, even Georgia could see, that she was right.

We'd eaten all we could eat of breakfast and were still digesting the news that we'd be living without adult supervision for an indefinite time when we noticed what a mess the kitchen was. Durinda had made a wonderful breakfast with Jackie's help, as good as Mommy would have made, but there were dirty dishes and a dirty griddle, and pancake batter was splattered all over the counters, cabinets, and floor.

"Right, then," Annie said, "while Marcia, Petal, Zinnia, and I dress to tackle shoveling the walk, Georgia and Rebecca can clean up the kitchen."

"That's not fair!" Georgia said. "We cleaned the litter boxes!"

"Yes," Annie said, "but Durinda and Jackie made breakfast. It wouldn't be fair to ask them to clean up too. Besides, before you know it, we'll be needing lunch, and then dinner—Durinda will have to see to that as well."

We all thought about that, and even Georgia had to admit: it was fair.

"Before I become a scullery maid," Georgia said, "is it possible to ask a question?"

"Of course," Annie said.

"Who died and left you boss?"

"Hopefully, no one died," Annie said. "But someone does need to take charge of organizing everything around here, and I am the oldest."

"Only by a minute," Georgia objected.

It was true. We'd each been born a minute apart, meaning that Annie was older than Durinda by only a single minute and older than the youngest of us, Zinnia, by only a whopping seven minutes. If fate had been different, with just a two-minute switch, Georgia might have been the oldest, with Annie the third in the line. It was a time technicality that regularly annoyed Georgia.

"Fine, then." Annie paused, then spoke meaningfully. "Would *you* like the job?"

For a moment, we all thought Georgia might rise to the bait, and who knew what might happen then, or what Annie might do. But Georgia backed down with a muttered, "I still don't see why you get to tell everyone what to do. And how do you think we'll pull this off anyway?"

"We're eight!" Annie said. "We can do anything!"

"You're not *eight!*" Rebecca said. "None of us are!"

"Close enough," Annie said. "It is now officially 2008. On August eighth, we'll be eight. This is our eighth year on this planet. If people asked what year we were born, we'd say 2000, and they'd do the math and come up with eight. So why quibble?"

"Can I ask a question?" Zinnia's voice was timid.

"Of course," Annie said gently.

"It's just this," Zinnia said. "It's what you said before about Durinda making lunch and then dinner. There's plenty of food in the house now." This was true. Mommy had done what she always referred to as "a big shop" when we'd arrived home from Utah. We probably had enough food to last us a week or two. "But," Zinnia continued, "if this . . . goes on, what will we do when we run out of supplies?"

Annie shrugged. "I suppose one of us will have to learn how to drive."

"You never said before," Georgia said testily. "How long do we have to pull this off?"

Annie shrugged again. "As long as it takes."

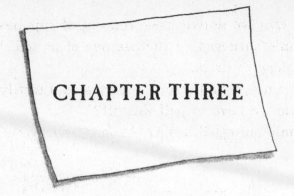

CHAPTER THREE

The rest of the day went uneventfully; well, as uneventfully as it could go without any parents in the house. Durinda took care of the food at every meal and Annie organized us about everything else. We still hadn't found our powers—or, if any of us had, we didn't know it—and we were certain we hadn't found any gifts. Could Durinda's ability to cook be considered a power? We didn't think so, but it definitely came in handy.

But the next morning found big changes. It was time to go back to school.

"Please don't make us go in the hair-cutting room!" Petal cried.

"Of course I won't," Annie said. "It's not my job to make any of you do anything that isn't necessary for our survival."

The hair-cutting room was one of our mother's

inventions, our least favorite. You sat in the chair, said what kind of hairstyle you wanted, and several sets of scissors flew around your head, wildly snipping away until the desired look was complete. It was a ritual: whenever we returned to school, we all had to get a trim. We mostly worried that when the desired look was complete, it would involve us missing our ears.

"But I could use a trim," Annie said of her own short hair.

We watched as she hopped into the cutting chair, put a smock on, and commanded the scissors, "Take a half inch off all around, please." The scissors flew around her head as Annie sat there bravely, unflinching.

"Voilà!" she said, tearing off the smock when the cutting was done.

Our mother always drove us to school, but that was impossible now. So Annie phoned the school's bus company. Imitating Daddy's voice again, she informed them that eight Huits would now be taking the bus.

The bus company must have objected to the short

notice, because we heard Annie say, sounding rather regal, "What do you *mean* I should have called you earlier about this change? Do you have any idea how much money I pay each year to keep *eight* children in that school?"

The bus company must have found Annie's argument persuasive because we saw her smile. "Jolly good," she said and hung up.

Then Durinda helped us arrange our hair the way we liked it and made us all put on our uniforms, which were plaid, plaid, and more plaid, and which we hated (although we suspected one of us loved it).

We'd always loved having Mommy drive us to school in her big purple vehicle, which was a Hummer that she'd doctored to make it environmentally sound, but riding the bus was a revelation.

"This is . . . fun," Zinnia said as we bounced along. "Who knew taking public transportation could be so . . . bouncy! It's so much more than yellow!"

Our school was called the Whistle Stop, a name we'd always agreed was stupid. But supposedly the man who had founded the school had made his fortune in railroads, and he liked the name. The lower school building, where we attended classes, was called the Station House.

The Whistle Stop ran kindergarten through twelfth

grade, and it was a private school. We were in third grade there because we were incredibly smart and had skipped a year right upon entry. This was a good thing for the other students in our class; without us, there would have been just two students in that grade. Apparently, there had been a year in which few children were born in our city, or at least few children whose parents wanted to send them to a private school stupidly named the Whistle Stop.

The other two students in our grade were Will Simms, a towheaded boy we liked very much because he was

always willing to get up to all manner of adventure with us, and Mandy Stenko, who we really didn't like at all but who we tried to be nice to because without us she would have had nobody. Mandy was a true redhead who tried to personalize her uniform by wearing little smiley and rainbow buttons on the lapel of her yellow plaid blazer. We had the feeling she didn't like us either.

Our teacher was Mrs. McGillicuddy, who was a tall blonde with a long nose, on the bridge of which perched horn-rimmed glasses. The McG, as we called her amongst ourselves, was also not a fan of the Sisters Eight.

"There, there, Phyllis," we'd overheard Principal Freud say to her early in the school year, the McG's bun askew. "What do you expect me to do—hire another teacher full-time so that poor person can get stuck with the eight while you have to teach only the two left? I'm sorry, but it's just not in the budget."

"But you don't understand!" the McG had cried. "They're not human!"

At the time, we could tell that even Principal Freud thought this was a bit much. It wasn't like we had done anything to our new teacher, not yet, not really. Yes, there had been that one toad incident, and we could tell it bothered the McG whenever Marcia corrected her grammar. But you couldn't blame poor Jackie for the toad thing—it's practically expected of third-graders, isn't it?—and Marcia couldn't help it if she was really good at grammar or that the McG's own grammar was, well, lousy.

But here we were, back in school on the second day of January, and things were going great. Will was there (which was not always the case since he tended to get sick a lot); Mandy had yet to say anything mean; and the McG had yet to muddle her grammar, so Marcia had yet to correct her. It was a happy time.

And then that all changed.

The McG wanted to have that talk teachers always have the first day back at school: What Did You Do on Your Vacation?

That part went innocently enough.

"I was sick the first half," Will said, "but then I got better and I got to go ice-skating. That half was really great."

"*My* family went skiing on the Matterhorn," Mandy said. Then for good measure, just in case we had somehow missed the fact that she was living a higher life than the rest of us were, she fluffed her hair.

"We got snowbound in Utah," Durinda said.

"How awful," the McG said, adding, "for your parents."

Thankfully, the idea of being snowbound by a blizzard was exciting enough to the others that we didn't have to say anything else about our vacation, like, say, how our parents had gone *poof!*

There was a lengthy pause. Then the McG said, "Isn't anyone going to ask *me* how *I* spent my time off?"

"Of course, Mrs. McGillicuddy," Petal said kindly. "We care."

"I rested," our teacher said. "I had a huge headache and I rested."

A headache? *For seventeen days?* Surely, she wasn't blaming *us* . . .

We were forced to endure a moment of silence in honor of the pain the McG had suffered. The bad part came when she broke the silence by saying, "Now, tell me, what did all you good children get for Christmas?"

"I got a new set of hockey skates and a stick," Will said.

"I got a walkie-talkie, binoculars, and a book on how to conduct covert surveillance," Mandy said with another hair fluff, "and a doll."

"And what did you get, Eights?" the McG prompted.

"We didn't get anything for Christmas," said Durinda.

"*Nothing?*" The McG was openly shocked. "But, surely, even you Eights couldn't have been so awful as to get *nothing.*"

"We weren't awful," Jackie piped up. "We were just Jewish."

"Ex*cuse* me?" the McG said.

"We're Jewish," Jackie said simply, lying with ease. "We don't celebrate Christmas because we're Jewish."

"I'm quite certain," the McG said, "you are not. I distinctly remember your parents singing carols louder than anybody at the holiday sing-along. And I remember all of *you* talking about the gifts you wanted."

"Oh," Annie said, covering for Jackie, "we only did that to make everyone feel better. We didn't want to make everyone else feel as if they had to do something special for us, like sing 'The Dreidel Song.'"

"No, but—" the McG started to say, but Will cut her off.

"Oh, but they are," Will said. He really was a miraculous boy. "They are very Jewish. I know. I've seen it for myself. I've been to their house."

"What are you talking about, William?" demanded the McG.

He *had* been to our house, many times, but we wondered too: what *was* he talking about?

"Their house." Will gave a slight nervous cough. "There are menorahs and, like, Stars of David . . . everywhere! They even have those mezuzah thingies, and they all wear yarmulkes. You can barely move in the place for all of that stuff. Honestly, the Eights are more Jewish than a rabbi!"

"Shalom," Jackie said for good measure.

"Mazel tov," Petal said.

"Gesundheit," Rebecca said with a sneer.

The McG looked at Will, stunned.

We were stunned too. Why had Will, who was always so painfully honest, lied on our behalf?

"Why, Will?" Annie asked, when we all went to recess. "Why did you lie to the McG for us?"

"I dunno." Will shrugged, as though even he wasn't sure. "Maybe I did it because you looked like you needed saving right at that moment, like it was really important to you somehow." He shrugged again. "Maybe I just did it because you're the Eights."

We all fell in love with him a little bit at that moment.

* * * * * * * *

The rest of the school day passed without major event, and we're sorry to say, the bus ride home was not as exciting as the earlier one. Apparently, the charms of mass transportation wear off quickly, even with the bounces.

When we got home, Petal and Zinnia raided the cabinets for cookies, while Georgia and Rebecca fought over what we should watch on TV.

The Summer Room, where we watched TV, was one of four seasonal rooms at the back of the house. The

front room, decorated normally, was for your average visitor. But the four seasonal rooms were for us. Mommy had created the rooms because she wanted us always to be able to go to the season we most wanted to be in when we grew tired of the one we were living. Well, we certainly didn't need the Winter Room now.

"What do you think you're doing?" Annie shouted over the roar of all of us.

"Eating cookies and watching TV, of course," Marcia said simply, popping a whole cookie into her mouth.

"But that's not what we *do* right after school," Annie said sternly. "We always do our homework first, in order to make sure it gets done."

"But those are Mommy's and Daddy's rules," Georgia

said, "and they're not here anymore."

"Yes," Rebecca said. "There has to be *some* advantages."

"Well, this isn't going to be one of them." Annie snapped off the set. "Durinda, make a healthy snack for the girls—I'm thinking apple slices and glasses of milk—while the rest of you get out your schoolbooks."

"You're worse than Mommy and Daddy," Georgia said. "At least they smile when they say those things."

"Can't we play in the snow first?" Zinnia asked. "It'll be dark soon, and the bus ride was so long."

"No," Annie said. "Work first. We can always turn on the outside lights if there's time to play outdoors afterward."

"Sheesh," Georgia said. Then: "Before I start my homework," she offered sweetly, "can I go get the mail for you? We forgot to pick it up. Maybe there are holiday cards waiting out there or even another important note telling us what to do about Mommy and Daddy."

"Thank you, Georgia," Annie said. "That would be lovely. It's nice to see you finally getting into the spirit of things."

We were all busy attacking our math homework, Annie at the head of the table supervising, when Georgia returned a few minutes later. She had a huge stack of mail in her hands.

Annie looked up from helping Zinnia. "Anything interesting?"

Georgia walked right up and dropped the envelopes on the table in front of her, one at a time.

"What's all this?" Annie asked.

"Bills, I believe they're called," Georgia said, with a smile that could almost be called evil.

"And what do you expect me to do with them all?" Annie asked, looking overwhelmed.

"I expect you to find a way to pay them, of course," Georgia said. "You did want to be in charge of everything, didn't you?"

And that's when Annie started to scream.

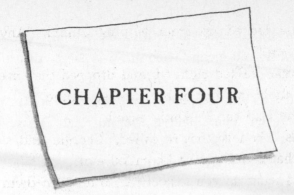

CHAPTER FOUR

"I can't do it!" Annie ran from the room. "I can't do it!" Her voice echoed back as she raced through the house, away from us.

"What came over her?" Georgia asked.

"*You* did," Jackie said with rare venom.

"How do you mean?" Georgia was the picture of innocence.

"What do you imagine it must be like," Jackie said in a more even tone, "having Mommy and Daddy disappear—"

"But that happened to all of us," Rebecca objected on Georgia's behalf.

Jackie went on as though Rebecca hadn't spoken. "And then be the one who has the most pressure on her to get everything *right,* the most pressure to fix everything so the rest of us remain okay?"

"I can't do it!" Annie cried, running into the room and then out again, a crazed look in her eyes.

Georgia shrugged. "Annie wanted to be in charge and now she is. I don't see how any of that's my fault."

"Great," Jackie said. "You don't *see.* But what do you think will happen to the rest of us if Annie does give up? How long do you think it will be before everything falls apart and we get split up?"

"She has a point," Rebecca said.

"Yes, I do see that," Georgia said.

"Good." Jackie nodded. "Now, what are you going to do about it?"

"Lead an ambassadorial delegation?" Georgia suggested.

So that's what we did. With Georgia in the lead, we

hunted through the house until we at last found Annie. She was sitting in Daddy's study. The lights were out in there, so we couldn't see her at first, but we knew she was there because we could hear her sobbing.

Durinda switched on the lights, illuminating the soothing golden-orange walls of the room, and there was Annie in Daddy's oversize blood-red leather chair, her forehead pressed down on the great big mahogany desk as though she might never lift it again.

"Annie?" Georgia took a few cautious steps forward. Okay, we pushed her. "I wanted to apologize. I'm not sorry I brought you the bills. After all, if we don't pay them, we'll have no lights, heat, or phone, and we'll starve. But I am sorry I brought them to you in such a nasty way."

It was a long speech for Georgia, who was more given to nasty snippets. It even sounded as though she were sincere.

Just then a carrier pigeon with a poor sense of how close it was to the nearest object smashed up against the window behind the desk. It was one of Daddy's friends,

of course. Why else would it come to Daddy's study? When Daddy was at home, he was often visited by carrier pigeons.

Durinda opened the window and the pigeon hopped onto her finger.

"Check to see if there's a note attached to its leg," Jackie advised.

Durinda unfurled the tiny scroll she extracted from the silver tube attached to the pigeon's leg, but it was empty except for a single red letter that could have been an *M* or a *W* or even a funny *E* or a *3*.

"What should I do?" Durinda asked.

"Send a note back." Jackie shrugged. "It's what Daddy always does."

But none of us had any idea what Daddy put in those notes.

We are all fine here, Durinda wrote. *No need to worry.*

"Shouldn't you be putting *SOS* in that instead?" Rebecca wondered.

"No, I shouldn't." Durinda let the pigeon go. "We want the world to think we're okay here, don't we?" Then she shut the window.

"We need you," Georgia went on softly to Annie, who had completely ignored the advent of the pigeon. "We can't do anything without you."

"It's true." Petal let out a slight sob. "Without you, we'd be orphans."

"We *are* orphans," Rebecca corrected, holding up her end of the testiness Georgia had dropped for the time being, "practically."

"Please, Annie," Georgia half begged, slitting open the envelope of one of the bills, "won't you just look at one of these little bills? I'd do it myself, but I can't make heads or tails of it. 'Minimum balance due,' 'total balance due'— how is a person to know which one to pay?"

Why, we wondered, hadn't our mother invented an automatic bill-paying system? We knew some people paid their bills by computers, but Mommy didn't wholly trust computers.

"And look," Marcia said, holding up a gray and white puffball. "Anthrax is here too, and I'm sure she'll sit at your feet for as long as you need her." Marcia held Anthrax up; we could all hear her purr.

Annie still hadn't spoken, but at the sound of Anthrax's purr, she forced her forehead off the desk and looked at us. Tears streaked her face. It was horrible to see Annie looking like that.

Angrily, she wiped the tears from her cheeks. Then, with a weary sigh, as though she were the oldest person in the world and not just in this house, she held out her hand.

We wondered, did she want us to hand her the cat?

But she snapped her fingers and then pointed at the bill in Georgia's hands. "Let me see it," she commanded. "I can at least look."

Now that Georgia had what we had wanted, she looked hesitant. Perhaps she was worried that when Annie looked at the bill, she'd have another breakdown and run screaming into another room.

But at last, with a tiptoeing step followed by a hasty retreat, Georgia deposited the bill into Annie's hand.

Annie studied it for a moment without speaking, and we studied Annie.

"I think I'll ride the car for a bit," Petal announced nervously.

Petal wasn't referring to the car in the garage. She was referring to the miniature pink convertible that had been one of our gifts on our sixth birthday. The rest of us had long since outgrown it. Not Petal, though. She still liked to tool around in it whenever she was nervous about something.

"Fine," Annie said, waving her away. She was still thinking, studying the bill. Then a smile broke across her face.

"This is easy!" she said. "If we don't want to pay it all, the minimum balance is the least amount we can pay without getting in trouble. But look at this rate here. If we don't pay the entire balance, they want 19.4 percent interest—that's usury! They're crooks!"

None of the rest of us knew what usury was, but from the look on Annie's face, we could tell it wasn't anything good.

"But how do we know if we can afford to pay it all?" Durinda asked. "How can we pay any of the bills Georgia delivered?"

"*I* didn't make the bills come!" Georgia objected as Petal zipped in and out of the room in her car. "It was that wretched mailperson who—"

But Annie cut her off with another snap-point of her fingers. "Georgia." Snap-point. "You get me the rest of the bills and then hand them to me one at a time as I tell you to. Zinnia." Snap-point. "Get me a pen. Jackie." Snap-point. "You get me the calculator. Rebecca." Snap-point. "Go to Mommy and Daddy's bedroom and get the strongbox. Remember they always said to grab it in a fire? Well, I'll bet anything the money stuff is in there. Petal." Snap-point. "You keep riding your car."

We all ran to do her bidding. But for once our actions weren't grudging. We were happy to help, even Rebecca; happy to be told what to do.

When we returned with the things she'd asked for,

Annie opened the strongbox and discovered a black leather ledger. It was the checkbook.

"This is exactly what I wanted!" she said. "Now, if only there's enough money in here to keep the bill collectors from the door for another month."

"What if we're broke?" Petal stopped her driving long enough to ask. "We'll have to pick pockets like those street urchins in that movie *Oliver!* Mommy had us watch."

"I'll bet I could pick a pocket or two," Rebecca said.

Annie opened the ledger very slowly, as though scared to see what was there. Well, who could blame her? What if we really were broke?

But then another huge smile spread across her face and she laughed out loud.

"What is it?" Georgia, now seated in a chair to the right of Annie's desk, asked anxiously. We were all worried our sister had gone nuts.

"We're rich!" Annie said.

"We're rich?" Zinnia was puzzled, as were we all. "What did Mommy and Daddy do for a living to make us all rich?"

"Don't you remember?" Annie said. "Daddy was a model and Mommy was a scientist."

"Huh. Really?" Zinnia asked. "I thought Mommy just

cooked and cleaned and Daddy read books."

"Where do you think all these inventions came from?" Annie asked. "They were all Mommy's from, you know, being a scientist."

"Who knew," Durinda said with wonder, "that there could be so much money in modeling and science?"

"Durinda." One last snap-point. "You go prepare the biggest feast you've made yet." Annie rubbed her hands together, then picked up a pen. "I have a feeling that when I'm done here, I'll be very hungry."

And then Annie got to work.

First, she practiced Daddy's signature. At the end of fifteen minutes, her forgery wasn't perfect—it had too many stops and starts—but it was close enough that someone looking at it would probably only think the writer had a bad case of the sneezes that day.

Then Annie did as she'd said she would do, having Georgia hand her one bill at a time.

Every now and then, Petal would whiz through with a beep of her horn.

"This is easy," Annie said with glee, her fingers flying on the calculator. "I could do this all day."

"You're very good at it," Georgia said with real admiration, and then a light dawned in her eyes and *she* snap-pointed. "That's *it!*" she cried.

"What's it?" Annie briefly looked up from her work, then put her head down to the task once more, muttering, "I'll tell you one thing: there will be no more paying the minimum balance in *this* household. I refuse to give the usurers the satisfaction." She looked at Georgia, who was bouncing excitedly in her seat.

"That's *it!*" Georgia said again.

"What's it?" Annie said again.

"Your power!" Georgia said with glee. "Your power! *This* is your power!"

"The calculator?" Annie asked, confused.

"No!" Georgia said breathlessly. "Although I must admit, you are very good at it. But no, what I meant was, your power is to be smart!"

"But I've always been smart."

"Perhaps," Georgia conceded. "But not like this. Two weeks ago, you were happy enough watching cartoons on TV and dreaming up ways to short-sheet my bed. But now look at you! You're running a whole household! You're keeping us in line! You're using a calculator! You're forging signatures! You're balancing a checkbook!" She paused, as though hearing a drumroll. *"You're managing household finances!"*

Annie sat up a little straighter. "I suppose I am doing those things."

"You are," Georgia went on enthusiastically, "and

you're doing them *splendidly.* This is your power: you're smarter—a *lot* smarter—than you once were. Why, if you weren't only seven, you'd be an adult!"

"I don't know what to say." Annie blushed. Then: "But what kind of lame-o power is that, being smarter than I once was?"

"It's a *fantastic* power," Georgia said. "It may not be glamorous or exotic, like seeing through walls or making people go invisible. But being as smart as an adult? That's the exact power we all need for you to have right now. It's the best power you could have."

"Well, when you put it like that. . . . *Say.*" Annie's eyes lit up. "If I have my power, and it was here all along, do you think my *gift* might also be lying around the house and I don't even know it?"

"Like, where were you thinking of looking?" Georgia asked with interest, although some of the glimmer had left her eyes.

"I dunno." Annie shrugged. "Maybe it's behind that loose stone in the drawing room, where we found the original note?"

"Don't be daft," Georgia scoffed. "Do you really think it's going to be that easy? Every time we move that rock—*whoops!*—there's a gift?"

"Well." Annie shrugged again. "It would be nice if it worked that way."

Despite her scoffing, Georgia followed Annie to the drawing room and watched as Annie removed the stone from the wall. Georgia was right in that there was nothing you could call a gift in the darkness behind the stone, but Annie was right also: there was *something* there.

There was another note.

Dear Annie,

Nice work discovering your power.
And since you're good at math now,
I'm sure you can follow along with
me when I say: one down, fifteen
items to go.

Again, the note was unsigned.

"What do you suppose it means?" Georgia asked.

"It means that there are eight of us and we each need to find two items: a power and a gift. Eight times two makes sixteen. I found my power, so that takes away one item, leaving fifteen items to find."

"I'm glad you're so good with math," Georgia said, "but what else does it mean? How did the note get there? Who put it there? How does that person know you found your power? Is that person here now?"

"I dunno," Annie said. "The original note that appeared on New Year's Eve—there was never any evidence that someone else was here, other than the note itself. Certainly, nothing bad happened to us that night—if you leave out Mommy and Daddy disappearing; certainly nothing like what you'd expect if, say, there were an ax murderer in the house."

"Then what does it all *mean?*" Georgia asked again, to which Annie shrugged one more time.

"I suppose," Annie said, "it means there's magic loose in the world."

CHAPTER FIVE

"You call it magic," Georgia said, "*I* call it spooky."

"Well, whatever we call it," Annie said, "it's not getting the bills paid."

Just then, Durinda called us. "*Dinner!* And hurry up! Do you think I slaved over a hot stove just to let the food go cold?"

"She's sounding more like a housewife every day," Georgia said.

"Can you blame her?" Annie countered.

The meal smelled great as we gathered in the kitchen. Annie told us about finding her power, and Georgia told us about finding the note. It felt like Christmas, if a person were allowed to celebrate that holiday properly ever again.

"Could you set the table?" Durinda asked robot Betty, who had wandered into the room. But instead of going for the silverware drawer, Betty picked up a dust rag and began dusting the stove.

"Never mind that," Durinda said. "Why don't you go watch some TV?"

Betty happily rolled out of the room; the robot loved to watch cartoons.

"I'll set the table," Jackie offered.

"What is this?" Annie lifted the silver dome off a serving platter and sniffed. "Turkey? How did you manage on such short notice?"

Durinda walked to the counter and held up a long box that was lying there. "It's not *a* turkey, not like one with legs and stuffing inside and things. It's this frozen precooked turkey loaf stuff that you reheat in the oven." She held up another box, this time a tall one. "And I found this instant stuffing in the cabinet. You just add water and heat. No shoving your hand inside a big greasy bird. Who knew Mommy was cutting culinary corners?"

"And the mashed potatoes?" Annie prompted, passing that plate.

Durinda waved a masher in the air. "Easy."

"Well," Annie said, "it all looks great."

Durinda blushed, clearly pleased with herself.

"Perhaps," Annie said, "one of us should say grace? Zinnia?"

We all bowed our heads over our clasped hands as Zinnia spoke.

"Thank you . . ." She paused. "Who should I thank?"

"Thank the universe," Annie advised. "Why not go for broke? At least you'll know you've covered everything."

"Thank you, Universe," Zinnia went on, "for this wonderful hot meal, and thank you for Annie finding her power. May we all find the other fifteen items." She paused again. "That's all, I think."

Dinner was very festive that night for the first time since Mommy and Daddy's disappearance. Talk flowed easily like conversation; juice boxes flowed like water—it was as though we were a real family once again, even if there weren't any adults in the house.

Durinda brought in the pumpkin pie and a can of whipped cream—"The refrigerator says we're out of whipped cream after this," she informed us, shaking the can—when for the first time Annie noticed a lone envelope beside her place setting.

"What's this?" she asked. "Another bill?"

"I don't think so," Georgia said, wiping her mouth with a linen napkin. One day soon, we would need to figure out how to use the washer and dryer in the laundry room. "I left it when you asked me to get all the bills, because I was fairly certain this one *wasn't* a bill. See? The address is handwritten. I'm fairly certain they don't handwrite bills these days."

"Unless of course their computer broke down," Annie grumbled.

But it wasn't a bill. It was an invitation.

"Will Simms is having his birthday party two weeks from Saturday!" Annie announced. "It's to be held at Kids' Castle!"

"This is just what we need," Petal said with a happy laugh, "something to take our mind off our troubles."

"I forgot Will's birthday was coming up," Jackie said. "How could I?"

"Never mind that," Rebecca said. "How will we get there? It's miles away and still freezing out—if we walk, by the time we get there, we'll be Popsicles!"

"Never mind *that* even," Georgia said. "How will we ever get to the stores to buy him a present? We can't very well arrive empty-handed. Maybe if it was Mandy Stenko we could do that, but not for Will Simms."

"If we can't walk," Zinnia said, "how will we get to either place? We can't fly, can we?" She turned to Annie. "You have your power now. It doesn't by any chance include the ability to fly us places, does it?"

Just to humor her, to humor all of us, Annie gave a few feeble waves of her arms, as though they were wings. But flap as she might, she remained rooted to her chair.

"Sorry," she said at last. "'Fraid not."

"Taxi?" Jackie suggested hopefully. "Perhaps we could call a taxi?"

"If you find a taxi that can hold all eight of us plus the driver, let me know," Annie said. "In the meantime, however, that's no solution."

"Then we can't go," Petal said, tears forming in her eyes.

"Don't be ridiculous." The gentle hug Annie gave Petal was the opposite of her stern words. "If we don't go, the only person he'll have there will be Mandy, and then what kind of party would that be for Will?"

"But how will we get there then?" Marcia asked.

"Give me time," Annie said. "You can't expect me to pay bills and solve transportation problems all in one day. But I'll think of something."

* * * * * * * *

A week went by.

It was a week in which we settled into our new routine: letting Durinda do our hair in the morning, eating the breakfast she made, riding the bus to school, avoiding detection by the McG.

Every Tuesday, red folders were sent home that contained Important Papers from school. Sometimes these Important Papers required a signature or even a call to the school from a parent, which Annie handled with ease. Annie was turning into an ace forger and impersonator.

And the rest of our routine: playing, chores, homework. Sometimes we balked at the last, but Annie told us smart people had a greater chance of taking over the world than stupid ones, and we liked that idea. Plus, if we took over the world, we wouldn't have to go to school.

And so we worked, ate, played, bathed, tucked one another in, kissed one another good night, went to bed. Then we got up and did it again. Amen.

With Saturday came the sound of howling cats. They wanted to be fed. When we went to do so, we saw there was hardly any cat food left in the house.

"Almost out of cat food, we still need to get a present for Will and figure out how to get to his party next week, and soon we'll be out of human food too." Annie gave a deep sigh. "There's only one thing left for it." She gave another sigh at the sound of loud, thumping footsteps. "And would you please get down from climbing the walls, Petal."

Petal was indeed climbing the walls, and she was doing it in her wall-walkers. We'd each received a pair from our parents on our last birthday. The wall-walkers were an improvement on the bouncy boots Mommy had invented in that they could be used in any room in the house, not just the  drawing room. They'd been too big for our feet when we first got them, but they fit perfectly now, the suction cups on the bottoms sticking to the walls so nicely we could even walk on the ceiling if we wanted to.

"Sorry," Petal said sheepishly, coming back down.

It was Zinnia's turn to sigh. "I wonder what we would have gotten for Christmas this year if we *had* gotten our presents." Another sigh. "I'll bet whatever it was, it would have really been *something*."

Disregarding this, Annie phoned Information; we heard her ask for the number for Pete's Repairs and Auto Wrecking.

"God," she said as she waited for her call to ring through, "I hate those automated voices they use these days."

At last, she was connected.

"Hullo, Pete?" Annie used her Daddy voice. "Robert Huit here. Listen, I've got a problem with the old Hummer, a real sticky wicket . . . No, of course I'd bring it in, but the blasted thing won't even start . . . No, I don't want to call a towing place. They're all usurers, you know . . . Yes, yes, I know it's Saturday. But could you make a house call? I'll pay double . . ."

"What did he say?" Marcia asked breathlessly as Annie hung up.

"He said he'd be here in an hour." Annie was clearly pleased as punch with herself. "And he wanted to know why I call him 'old chap' now."

When the doorbell rang an hour later, Annie was ready. She'd prepared a blank check, signed it, and had it waiting on the table by the front door.

Pete was everything you would expect in a mechanic: incredibly tall, with a pepper-colored mop of hair that had some salt dusting the fringes, like snow on the sides of a paved street. He wore an old navy blue T-shirt that didn't fit properly; his large stomach played peekaboo over the top of his belt, to which were attached useful-looking tools. His boots had stains on them—

Mommy would never have let him inside—and his jeans hung so low that if he turned around, we could see the top of his bottom.

"Hey, Eights," he said, nodding at the rest of us standing behind Annie. We'd never been formally introduced, but we were the only octuplets in town and everyone knew who we were, even if we didn't always know who they were. "Is your daddy around?"

Pete had a nice smile, although there were lots of silver and gold fillings in it, and his eyes were dancing blue chips. As for his breath and general aroma, what can we say? Every time he opened his mouth to speak or moved a muscle, a wave came off him like the rubbing lotion Mommy put on Zinnia's chest whenever she got a bad cold.

"Of course he's around," Annie said with all the authority she could muster. "He called you, didn't he?"

Pete couldn't deny that.

"But right afterward," Annie went on, "he was felled by a terrible virus."

"It's true." Jackie backed up Annie. "He's been in the, um, *bathroom* ever since he phoned you. You wouldn't want to see him right now."

"And our mother's not here," Zinnia piped up. "She's in, um, er, *France*."

"Oh." Pete turned away. "I guess I'd better come back another day."

"Oh, no. No, no, no," Annie said with a nervous laugh, reaching out to stop him. "Why waste another trip"—and here she picked up the check and waved it invitingly— "when Daddy left you a blank check right here?"

Pete had been made to see reason.

"Fine, then, Eights," he said. "Lead me to the beast that doesn't roar."

"What's he talking about?" Rebecca muttered.

"He means the car that won't start," Annie hissed at her.

We led Pete out to the cold garage and Mommy's purple Hummer.

"Ooh, here are the keys." Annie produced them. "Do you need them?"

"Usually," Pete said, accepting Annie's offering. "Thanks."

As Pete climbed into the driver's seat, Annie climbed into the passenger's side, indicating that the rest of us should climb in the back.

"Come on, um, *Eights,*" she said. "If we all watch what Mr. Pete does, then later we can tell Daddy all about how brilliantly he fixed it."

As Pete proceeded to do something with the key, Annie proceeded to narrate for us. Loudly.

"Now Mr. Pete is putting the key in the starter thingy and turning it. At the same time, he's pressing his right foot down on the far right pedal."

The engine roared into life.

"Huh," Pete said. "It started right up. Nothing wrong with the ignition."

"No?" Annie said nervously. "I know. Why don't you ride it around the block a few times to make sure there's nothing else wrong. I'm sure Daddy never would have called you if there wasn't something wrong."

Before Pete could object to her line of reasoning, Annie pressed the garage-door opener.

"Drive," Annie commanded.

And drive Pete did.

"Mr. Pete is putting it in something called *R,*" Annie narrated, "when he wants to go backward . . .

Now he's putting it in *D* and turning it around . . .
He's still in *D* as he starts to go faster . . . He does
a lot of spinning of the wheel and looking in various
mirrors . . . When Mr. Pete needs to stop, he hits the
left pedal . . ."

After going once around the block, we arrived back
in our driveway.

"Well, that all seems easy enough," Annie let out
without meaning to.

Pete put the car back in the garage and turned the
key again.

"To stop the car completely," Annie said, "Mr. Pete
is putting it in *P*, then turning the starter off and
taking the key—"

"Just what exactly is going on here?" Pete asked.

"How do you mean?" Annie asked, her eyes the
picture of innocence.

"This car. There's nothing wrong with it." He may
have had a poor fashion sense and smelled like rubbing lotion, but Pete wasn't stupid.

"Our father called you, didn't he?" Annie laughed
brightly, nervously.

"Give him the check," Georgia muttered.

"Right," Annie said, still brightly, "the check. How
much?"

"Nothing," Pete said.

"How is that possible?" Annie wondered.

"I can't charge you when I didn't do anything," Pete said simply.

"But you did something," Annie said. "You drove around the block!"

"Right," Pete said slowly. "But anyone could have done that. Your mother or father could have done that."

"Except," Rebecca said, "that our father is in the bathroom, very sick."

"Right, right," Pete said. "And your mother is in France." Pause. Then: "Can I speak with your father for a few minutes before I go?"

"Jackie," Annie directed, "go see if Daddy's free yet."

Jackie raised her eyebrows at Annie questioningly.

"*Now,*" Annie ordered.

So Jackie scurried off. A moment later we heard the sound of a toilet flushing. Several times. And then Jackie was back with us. Alone.

"Sorry," she said to Pete, "but Daddy says he's in no condition to see you right now." Again the toilet flushed. How had Jackie done that? Had she rigged the toilet? Or got one of the cats to help? "He's still, er, *busy.*"

"It could be contagious," Petal added seriously. "We

wouldn't want anything to happen to you, Mr. Pete."

He looked at all of us closely. It was like he knew something was up . . . but had no idea what.

"If that's the way it's going to be," he finally said. Then he reached into his tattered jeans and fished out a wrinkled business card. It said *Pete's Repairs and Auto Wrecking* and had a phone number on it.

"Look," he said, handing the card to Annie, "if you ever need any help with anything—if, you know, your dad doesn't come back from the toilet or your mom never comes back from, um, *France*—give me a call, okay?"

"Oh . . . sure," Annie said. "But that won't happen. Everything's just fine here. Well . . . thanks!"

* * * * * * * *

A few minutes later, we watched as Pete's van backed out of the driveway, and we all gave a collective sigh of relief.

"That was close," Durinda said. "He definitely suspected something."

"True," Marcia said. "We've discovered a chink in our armor. When we're out in the world, we can fake things okay enough, but if someone comes here—well, we don't do so hot. We act too nervous."

"I can't argue with that," Annie said, "but even though Pete suspects something's not quite perfect here, he doesn't really *know* anything. And besides . . ." Her voice trailed off.

"Yes?" Rebecca prompted.

"Something very valuable came out of the day," Annie said.

"And that is?" Rebecca prompted again.

Annie smiled. "Now we know how to drive a car." She paused and thought about it. "Well, sort of."

CHAPTER SIX

Annie stuck Pete's card to the fridge with a magnet, and it was as though it acted like a good angel, watching over our home. This peaceful state lasted all too briefly.

We awoke on Sunday to Annie ripping off our bedcovers and announcing, "Today we will go shopping!"

This caused a flurry of excitement. For the first time in more than two weeks we would be leaving our home to go somewhere other than school, and we would get there using something other than a bus or our feet.

"Where are we going to go?" we repeatedly asked while hurriedly brushing our teeth, putting on clothes, gulping our breakfast.

But Annie, drinking a cup of coffee—a new habit she had started that day and one that caused her to make funny faces—wouldn't say at first.

"The mall?" Rebecca guessed.

"Too common," Annie said.

"The great big drugstore where they also sell toys?" Zinnia guessed.

Annie looked down her nose so sharply, she might have been the McG. "Would *you* like to get your birthday present from a place where they sell toothbrushes and bad-tummy medicine?"

She made a good point.

"Where, then?" Jackie asked. "We could make Will something . . ."

"Don't be ridiculous," Annie said. "You know we'd never be able to agree on what to make. Petal would want to make him something like paper flowers, while Georgia would want to make him a miniature guillotine."

"But that could work," Marcia said, pouring Annie a second cup of joe. "Will would wind up with two presents instead of just one. And anyway, he could always dead-head the paper flowers with the guillotine."

"Perhaps," Annie conceded. "But I have something grander in mind."

We leaned forward breathlessly. "What?"

"The Grand Emporium of Children's Delights," Annie said.

We each let out a gasp.

The Grand Emporium of Children's Delights was one of the biggest toy stores in the world, rumored to have everything any child could want.

"We've never been there before!" Rebecca said.

"I've always wanted to go!" Zinnia squealed.

"Mommy always said that that sort of excess is bad for children," Marcia observed. Which was true, and which was why we had never been there.

"Well"—Annie winced at a gulp of coffee, then winked—"we're going now."

But first she said we had to help her get ready.

"If I'm to be the driver," Annie said, and none of us argued with her that she *shouldn't,* "then I'll need a disguise. We certainly don't want people all over town calling the police to inform them there's an eight-year-old driving a Hummer."

We didn't bother to correct her and say that she wasn't eight yet, none of us were, and the day we would be eight was still nearly seven months away. We were too excited for quibbles.

"Do you want me to go get your spear?" Rebecca asked.

"I don't think," Annie said, "that my riding around with a medieval weapon in my hand would do anything to deflect nosy people's suspicions. No, I was thinking along the lines of something subtle . . ."

Which was how we all found ourselves in the tower room, which in happier times was our playroom, going through our old costume trunk.

Annie rejected princess costumes and a witch's costume, which disappointed Georgia, who had had her heart set on Annie being a witch.

Georgia was still grumpy over that when we reached the bottom of the trunk and Annie pulled out something that made her shout, "Perfect!"

The white shirt, skinny black tie, and black jacket were all one piece, and there was separate dark trousers. Annie wore it whenever we played wedding.

"I still look too much like me," she said to the mirror. "I'll need a hat."

Before any of us could go off to fetch her one, however, Anthrax strolled in with one of Daddy's hats on her head, the hat being much larger than the cat. Daddy had a huge collection of old-fashioned hats and we'd heard him refer to this one as a fedora.

"Thank you, Anthrax," Annie said, removing the hat from the cat.

"Have you noticed," Marcia observed, "that Anthrax is smarter than she used to be? It was as though she just *anticipated* what Annie needed was one of Daddy's hats, and she found the perfect hat at that."

"The other cats have told me," Zinnia said, "that

lately Anthrax is bossier than she used to be."

We wondered if the cats really talked to the Zinnia.

"Do you think," Georgia asked Annie, "your power is rubbing off on your cat?"

"I honestly couldn't say," Annie said, distracted, "but this disguise definitely still needs something . . ."

That was when Anthrax leaped into the trunk, made lots of rattling noises as though she were chasing her own tail or fighting with another creature, then emerged with something hairy clasped in her jaws.

"What's she got?" Rebecca reeled back. "Is that a rat?"

"No, it's not a rat," Annie said with a smile, bending down to take the hairy something from Anthrax's jaws. She patted Anthrax, then took the hairy something and attached it to her upper lip. It was a fake mustache, we saw, as she studied herself one last time. "It's perfection."

And it was.

"Prepare the car," Annie instructed Durinda. "It's time to roll."

* * * * * * * *

But preparing the car was easier said than done.

It was simple enough for Durinda to start the Hummer, per Annie's instructions, but a lot less simple for Annie to drive it.

"I can't see over the dashboard," Annie said.

So we all trundled back inside, looking for boosters. At last, we settled on Mommy's *Oxford English Dictionary* as being just the ticket, but it was so heavy Zinnia, Petal, and Jackie had to carry it out in separate volumes.

But once Annie could see over the dashboard, she could no longer reach the pedals.

"We'll just have to rig up some sort of device," Durinda suggested.

Annie was in no mood for reason.

"This is taking too long!" she said. "If I wait for you to rig up some sort of . . . *device,* it'll be dark. And I can't drive in the dark, not my first time!"

Her lip actually quivered at that last, as though she were on the verge of tears, which scared us very much.

"Fine," Durinda said soothingly. "I'll just get down here on the floor beneath your legs, like so,

and you tell me when you want me to hit the gas to go and hit the brakes to stop. Will that work?"

We can't say it worked like a charm, and the ride was hair-raising—we had to rely on Durinda blindly following instructions to "Give it more gas!" and "Hit the brakes!"—but at least it got us there.

"It's . . . *grand,*" Zinnia said with awestruck eyes, gazing upward.

"It's the most *amazingly* grand place I've ever seen!" Petal amended.

"Let's go inside," Annie said.

"Aren't you going to change first?" Rebecca said to Annie. "Didn't you bring any normal clothes to go shopping in?"

"No," Annie said.

"But you look ridiculous," Rebecca pointed out.

"Maybe." Annie smiled. "But there is method to my ridiculousness."

Once inside, we couldn't settle down to shopping for Will right away. There was too much to look at, too much to touch and no parent there to say, "Don't touch," too much to play with.

There was the jungle area, with oversize stuffed animals and a gorilla that was a story tall. There was the dollhouse area, fully equipped with child-size houses and dolls. There was the magic area, with everything you could want for turning a toad into a prince or an enemy into a toad.

"Is this pretty wand and book of potions in our budget?" Zinnia asked.

"'Fraid not today," Annie said gently. "Too bad. I imagine spells and potions would come in handy now." Then she hustled us to the third floor of the store, where they sold mostly boy things and which we thought would be boring but that totally was not.

"I'm thinking something involving bats and balls," Marcia said.

"I'm thinking something that makes lots of noise," Jackie said.

"And I'm thinking," Annie said, "that we need to get him something stupendous."

"But why?" Rebecca asked.

"Because," Annie said, "when he comes to our parties, he always brings us eight presents. He deserves something grand."

"Well, he likes hockey . . ." Jackie's voice trailed off.

And that's when we saw it.

The Super-Duper Faux-Hockey Mash-'Em Smash-'Em Reality Toy Kit.

"It's perfect!" Annie said.

As we studied the gigantic box with her, we realized

that it was. It had everything—its own facemasks and shin guards and hockey sticks—and it even came with its own miniature indoor rink and instructions on how to create a winter wonderland in the basement of any normal-size home.

"It really is perfect!" Durinda said. "Any boy would love one of these."

"Well, Will certainly would," Annie said.

"But who will he play it with?" Durinda asked. "Will's an only child."

Annie shrugged. "I'd be happy to play this with him after school sometimes, wouldn't you?"

We all agreed that would be the best.

But when it came time to go pay for it, we realized the box of the one on display was badly torn, so Annie went to find a salesperson to see if a nicer one could be found.

It was while we were waiting for her to return that disaster struck.

Jackie was investigating the kit for turning enemies into toads when she felt a long finger tap on her shoulder. Turning slowly around, she was horrified to see it was . . . the McG!

"Hello, Eight," the McG said to her. "What are you doing here?"

"M-m-m-me?" Jackie said. "What are *you* doing here?"

The McG waved something in her hand.

"Getting a present for Will," the McG said. "His birthday is coming up and I always try to get a little something for my good students."

We could see from the size of the object in her hand, the shape of a deck of cards but not as thick, that it really was a *little* something.

"You never said though," the McG said, "what are you all doing here?"

"Ohhhh." Jackie twisted her fingers together as she strained to think of something, deciding on the truth for once. "We're shopping for Will too."

"How lovely," the McG said. "And where are your poor parents?" The McG scanned the store, looking over the top of Jackie's head.

"They're modeling and in France," Jackie said quickly, sticking to part of the lie we'd tried out on Pete.

"They're both modeling in France?" The McG raised an eyebrow.

"No, of course not." Jackie laughed nervously. "Did I say that? I *meant* to say Daddy's modeling in France while Mommy is . . . Mommy is . . ."

"Mommy is looking for a salesperson to get a better one of these for Will," Rebecca put in, inspiration striking her as she saw Annie walking back. Rebecca indicated the hockey kit.

"My, that is an impressive toy," the McG said coolly while, behind her back, Georgia gestured for Annie to go hide. It wouldn't do for the McG to see Annie disguised as a man with no parents in sight.

"And where is Annie?" the McG asked, looking around again.

"She's . . . she's . . . she has a dreadful stomach virus," Jackie said, once again relying on the lie we'd told Pete, only this time applying it to a different family member.

"I see," the McG said. "And who is taking care of her if your father is modeling in France and your mother is here with you?"

We couldn't very well say Annie was home alone, could we? Then the McG would question our parents' fitness to parent us. So Jackie said the only thing anyone could say.

"Oh, Annie's here too," Jackie said brightly. "Mommy was going to take her to the bathroom *again* before going off to find that salesperson. Hmm, I wonder what could be keeping them?"

At the mention of Annie being in the store and ill, the McG's lip curled.

"I really have to go pay for this," she said hurriedly, waving the thin deck of cards again. "I've a lot to do today. Please give my best to your poor mother and tell Annie I hope she feels better. And, for God's sake, if she's still feeling badly tomorrow, tell her to stay home from school."

"Oh," Jackie said with a smile, relaxing now that the McG was hurrying away from us, "I'm sure Annie will be better by then."

* * * * * * * *

Once the McG was gone, it was safe for Annie to come back. She had secured a nicer hockey kit, and we made our way to the cash registers.

When it came time to actually arrange payment for our purchase, we saw that Annie had thought of everything. She pulled out one of Daddy's credit cards and offered it to the stunned sales clerk.

The woman in her red smock and badly dyed blond

hair looked at Annie in her suit, hat, and mustache.

But Annie refused to be stared down.

"What's the matter," Annie said in her Daddy voice, "haven't you ever seen a midget, old chap? You know, it is jolly rude to stare . . ."

In the end, the embarrassed clerk ran the credit card through the register, apologizing profusely as she handed Annie a pen and the credit card slip, on the bottom of which Annie forged *Robert Huit.*

Annie really had thought of everything.

On the way home, she even remembered to stop for kibble for the cats.

CHAPTER SEVEN

When we arrived back home, we decided we should celebrate the success of our first adventure out.

First, we got out many of our own toys and played as we hadn't done since before Mommy and Daddy's disappearance.

"Or death," as Rebecca dourly put in.

Then, when we grew tired of board games and dolls and bouncy boots and Yahtzee—Jackie kept winning—we decided to play dress-up. Raiding the trunk in the tower room again, we emerged with Marcia and Jackie as fairies, Petal and Zinnia as princesses, Georgia as a witch, Rebecca as a jester, and Durinda in one of Mommy's old ball gowns. We all decided that since Annie already had her costume on, she should keep it that way.

But it had been a long day, with lots of pressures and worries, and no sooner were we in costume than we realized we were famished.

"What's for dinner?" Georgia asked Durinda. "Can you make us another one of those turkey things?"

But Annie said it wouldn't be a celebration for Durinda if she had to work. For once, we could eat what we wanted and forget the wretched food pyramid.

The idea of eating what we wanted was almost too good to bear.

"Perhaps," Zinnia offered timidly, "Durinda could be persuaded to work just long enough to pop a frozen pizza into the oven for us?"

Frozen pizza may not sound exciting, but to us, after two weeks of Annie's insisting we eat balanced meals with fruits and veggies, it sounded like heaven.

"Oh, yes, please!" Petal and Jackie cried. "May we? May we?"

Seven of us voted for the pizza, and we got our wish, but one of us wanted something different.

"You did say we could have whatever we wanted, didn't you?" Rebecca said pointedly to Annie. When Annie nodded, Rebecca got a chair, climbed on the counter, and reached for the highest cabinet.

"Ta-da!" she said, producing a can of pink ready-to-spread frosting.

We suspected then that Rebecca had been waiting her whole life for our parents to disappear so that she could eat an entire can of pink frosting. Next thing you know, she'd be doing gymnastics on her bed.

This suspicion deepened when, having eaten more than half of the frosting, Rebecca got a case of the hypers, bouncing all around us as we tried to consume our frozen pizza. She wasn't even using bouncy boots.

Rebecca was flying down the banister of the staircase—she'd already swung from the chandelier in the dining room—when the doorbell rang.

"Who could that be?" Marcia asked. "No one ever rings our doorbell."

Since Rebecca was the only one standing, it was she who went to the door. She peeked through the curtained window, and there was a sight that was enough to put fear into any child.

It was a giant toadstool.

Well, not a real toadstool. It was a person shaped like a toadstool. The person was an adult, but short enough to be a child, with coal black eyes, a fright of spiky yellow hair, a very plump body, and short legs that looked like they couldn't run fast but could kick hard. The person had on khaki pants and a red shirt with polka dots—no coat, despite the cold.

"Oh, no!" Rebecca whispered back at us. "It's the Wicket!"

The Wicket was how we referred amongst ourselves

to our next-door neighbor Helena Wicket.

"What should I *do?*" Rebecca hissed.

"I'm afraid you'll have to let her in," Annie said. "Our lights are all on; she must know somebody is home."

So that's what Rebecca did: opened the door and let the Wicket in.

Once she was inside, we could swear she was practically as short as we were. And yet she was somehow very scary too.

"Which one are you, Eight?" the Wicket said to Rebecca.

"I'm Zinnia," Rebecca said.

"I'm Petal," Zinnia said.

"I'm Jackie," Georgia said.

It may not have been nice to fool her, but we had a theory about people like the Wicket: if they couldn't be bothered to get our names straight, treating us as though we weren't each an individual person in her own right, we certainly wouldn't help them out any.

"I'm An—" Jackie started to say, but the Wicket cut her off.

"That's enough," she said, raising a palm. "I don't need to know any more. I came to deliver this present to your parents."

For the first time, we noticed something in her other hand: an oblong pan with red and green crinkle wrap covering the top. It looked heavy.

"I have a fruitcake for them," the Wicket said importantly.

It gave off a horrid smell, causing us to try not to inhale.

"Oh," Annie said, then she paused. "My." When she resumed speaking, she spoke brightly. "Well. Here, let me take that from you."

But the Wicket held the pan out of reach.

"I prefer," she said, "to deliver it myself. I have been very concerned. Your parents always attend the Collinses' New Year's Day bash, but I did not see them this year. I've tried calling here, often, to make sure everything is okay, but no one answers the phone, nor is the machine on."

It was true. We'd stopped answering the phone because we'd discovered that most calls were nuisance calls. It was always telemarketers asking us stupid questions or people trying to sell us credit cards, which we really didn't need; we already had plenty of those.

"But what if whoever is connected with Mommy and Daddy's disappearance tries to contact us?" Petal had asked at one point.

To which Annie had replied, "I don't think it'll happen that way. Whoever that person is seems to favor communicating by leaving notes behind that loose stone in the drawing room."

In a house with eight people, it had been odd to hear the phone ring without anyone ever answering it. The phone seemed to get louder and louder sometimes, as though it were screaming, *Pick me up! Pick me up!* But after a while, we'd gotten used to hearing it ring, unanswered. We'd gotten used to our parents disappearing, and after that, we could get used to anything.

"You're so right," Annie said to the Wicket now, "and we're very sorry. We'll be sure to answer next time."

"That will be an improvement"—the Wicket paused, peering closely at Annie as though trying to make out which one of us she was—*"Petal."* What a mistake to make! "But I'd still like to speak with your parents."

"I'm afraid that's impossible," Annie said quickly.

"How so?" the Wicket demanded just as quickly. "I saw the car drive up a few hours ago and it never left again."

"Daddy is in France modeling," Zinnia piped up.

"And where is your mother?" the Wicket pressed. "Surely"—she surveyed our disorganized home, messed up during the course of our celebration—"surely you can't be here alone." Pause. "Without adult supervision."

We were tired of saying one of our parents had a tummy virus. If we kept saying that, our family would get a bad reputation in town. So instead, Annie said, "I'm afraid Mommy is too busy working to be disturbed right now. You know"—she paused meaningfully—"she *is* a scientist."

At that, the Wicket's ears perked up.

"Yes, I did know that," the Wicket said. She tacked on a smile. "Can you tell me what sort of project your dear mother is working on now?"

"Sorry, no," Annie said abruptly. "Top secret."

The Wicket looked disappointed. Then: "Do *you* know what it is?"

"'Fraid I can't answer that one way or the other," Annie said. "If I did, the thumbscrew guys'd have to come for me."

"I see . . . *Zinnia,*" the Wicket said.

"It's Marcia," Annie said.

"I thought you said Petal," the Wicket said quickly.

"Didn't I just say Petal right now?" Annie said. "I'm sure that I did."

"I'm sure . . ." the Wicket began. Then: "Never mind. So, your mother is working on something top-secretly scientific . . . in her office right now?"

We had to change the story fast. The way The Wicket was craning her neck around, we were sure if we said Mommy was in her study—for it was *a study* and not something so boring as *an office*—the Wicket would charge through us, moving like a greased pig, and then the jig would be up.

"No, actually," Annie said, "she's not."

"The thumbscrew guys snuck in earlier," Jackie put in. "Not because Mommy did anything wrong but because, you know: top secret. Cover of darkness, cone of silence. You probably didn't even hear their car drive up or see it—they're that good at covert operations."

"Then you *are* here alone?" The Wicket had an *ah-HA!* in her voice.

"Just briefly," Annie said. "Daddy will be coming home from France any time now. But," she hurried to add, "he'll be coming in the limo, and it's one of those very quiet limos, so you probably won't hear him. Also, he'll be very tired—you know, jet lag—so I'll just take that lovely fruit-cake from you now and see that he gets it."

"Perhaps I should stay with you," the Wicket said shrewdly, although she did let go her vise grip on the fruitcake. "You know, children really shouldn't be left unattended. Particularly not eight of them."

"You can see"—Annie indicated the wrecked room behind her—"we're managing just fine. And as I say, Daddy should be home any second—oops!" She cocked a hand behind one ear. "Do I hear a car now? You'd best go. If it is Daddy, he doesn't like to have visitors thrust upon him first thing. He just gets so tired. You know: jet lag. Modeling. *France.*"

Georgia and Rebecca each took the Wicket firmly by an elbow, and Jackie raced ahead to open the front door.

"But . . ." said the Wicket. "But . . . but . . ."

"Goodbye, Mrs. Wicket!" we all called after her as Georgia and Rebecca attempted to shove her out the door.

"But why are you dressed like that, Petal?" the Wicket finally demanded of Annie.

It was too late, though. Jackie had already slammed the door.

"I'm dressed as Daddy, you stupid cow," Annie muttered to the closed door. "We're children. We're playing dress-up."

"Well, that was no fun," Rebecca said, wiping her brow.

"And it'll get less fun," Annie said sternly. "That was a close call."

"That woman is evil," Georgia said with a shudder.

"But what can we do about her?" Marcia asked. "She lives right next door. And we can't very well move. Or ask her to move. I suppose a tall fence is out of the question too?"

"And she'll be back," Georgia warned, ignoring Marcia's last comment. "Her kind always are."

"We'll have to make it, then," Annie said, "so that she thinks Daddy did arrive back home tonight, to put her off the scent."

"But how?" Petal asked.

"First," Annie said, "I'm going to get rid of *this*." The *this* was the wretched fruitcake, which she offered to the cats, who refused it, before tossing it in the kitchen trash. "Now," Annie said, "follow me."

So we followed her into the drawing room, where she walked straight up to the suit of armor.

"Not the spear again." Georgia groaned.

"Do you mean to kill the Wicket?" Rebecca said in a hushed tone.

"No, not the spear," Annie said, "and we're not going to kill anybody." She thought about this, shrugged. "Well, not unless we have to."

Then she grabbed hold of the suit of armor, directing us to help.

"What are we going to do with Sparky?" Petal

asked, using our pet name for the suit of armor.

"Sparky's going on a little trip," Annie said.

So, following her instructions, we carried Sparky out to the front room, where Annie had us sit him down in a big comfy chair by the window. Then she drew the drapes and turned on the lamp behind the chair.

"There," she said, "anyone looking in will think a man is sitting here."

"Sparky doesn't look quite human, though," Marcia observed with a tilt of the head. "Not with that pointy helmet thing on."

So Annie relinquished her hat, putting it on Sparky's head. Then she went to the kitchen and fished around the junk drawer.

"There." Annie shoved the old corncob pipe we used when we made snowpeople into the gap in Sparky's facemask. "Daddy's home."

As if in response, Anthrax entered, hopping in Sparky's lap for a nuzzle.

"But our daddy doesn't smoke," Georgia said.

"He does now," Annie said with satisfaction. "In fact, I think I'll get Daddy's quilted smoking jacket for him, so he'll be more comfy."

"I'm exhausted," Rebecca said, the hypers having worn off some time ago.

"Me too," Georgia admitted. "How long are we going to have to keep this up, coming up with new charades to put off nosy parkers like the Wicket?"

"As long as it takes," Annie said. "As long as it takes."

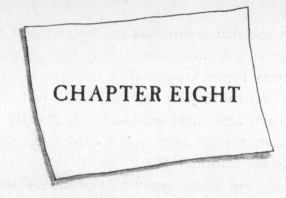

CHAPTER EIGHT

The next morning, still tired from our celebration and the Wicket worries of the night before, we walked downstairs to find the shock of Daddy Sparky still seated in the front window.

Yes, we had put him there ourselves, but he was still a shock.

And there was something sad about him.

"He looks so lonely there," Petal said, "sitting all by himself."

So then Annie got the idea that he *shouldn't* be alone. Even before breakfast, she had us all go back upstairs to Mommy's great big closet where she kept a wardrobe dummy. Besides being a scientist, Mommy was a great seamstress.

"Here." Annie selected a purple sleeveless dress and a string of pearls. "Let's dress Sally," she said, Sally being our name for the dummy.

Then she sent Durinda to the tower to get one of the wigs out of our costume trunk because she said the dummy looked silly bald.

Once we had the wig in place, Annie had us carry Sally downstairs. Then she had us stand Sally in the front room not far from where Daddy Sparky was enjoying his morning pipe.

"There," she said, satisfied, "now Daddy won't be lonely. What's more, when people look in from the outside, they won't wonder why they only see Daddy here but never Mommy."

"But," Rebecca pointed out, "won't they find it strange that Daddy is always sitting and Mommy is always standing?" The dummy was stiff.

"I suppose," Annie said, "they'll think Daddy is a man of leisure, which he somewhat is, being a model, and that Mommy waits on him hand and foot, which she never does."

"What about them always being in the same spot?" Rebecca asked.

"I'll devise a rotating schedule," Annie said. "We'll keep them in the front room in the mornings; it's nice to think of them chatting there after breakfast. But then we'll move them to other rooms: the drawing room in late afternoons for tea, the dining room for formal, and so forth. If they get too cold, we can always send them to the beach in the Summer Room."

So that's what we did. And thanks to Annie, we now had a mommy and daddy again. Well, sort of.

"Don't you think"—Rebecca had one last question—"people will think it odd that Mommy is wearing a summer dress in the middle of winter?"

"No, I don't," Annie said. "Everyone knows Mommy is a bit odd."

* * * * * * * *

Another school week went by, Annie in charge.

As the yellow cupcakes with chocolate frosting made the rounds at Will's in-school birthday celebration on Friday, the McG presented Will with her tidily wrapped gift. When he opened it up, we saw that she'd got him a deck of sports trading cards: soccer. Will didn't like soccer.

"Ooh," Georgia said. Annie kicked her under the table, encouraging her to be nice to the McG. "I've always loved soccer."

"Black and white balls," Rebecca added, not wanting to get kicked, "those have always been my favorite colors for balls."

"Soccer," Jackie observed with no kicking or threat

of kicking at all. "It's the wave of the future, isn't it?"

"I wish," Zinnia said with a sigh, "someone would give me soccer trading cards. Really, any present at all would do right around now."

"It's a terrific present," Will said to the McG stoutly. "Honestly, no one's ever given me anything quite like it before."

The McG beamed. Maybe, we thought, she wasn't so bad after all.

Then she told Annie not to touch the cupcakes, just in case she still had that stomach virus she had before, and we thought: Yes, she was that bad.

But so what if Annie hadn't been able to enjoy any of the frosting at Will's in-school birthday party? There was sure to be plenty of frosting on hand at his real birthday party at Kids' Castle the next day.

* * * * * * * *

The next morning we arose with greater excitement than we'd had on New Year's Eve morning. We were going to a party!

Too bad Annie made us all dress in dresses.

"It's what Mommy would have you do," she said when we objected.

"But it's Kids' Castle!" Georgia said.

"Besides," Rebecca added, "Mommy isn't here. Or Daddy."

"Doesn't matter," Annie said. "If she *were* here, she would tell us even scientists should look like ladies. Unless they're men, of course."

It was true, we couldn't deny it: Mommy would say that.

"What about you?" Rebecca sneered at Annie. "No dress?"

"I'm still the driver." Annie held up her Daddy disguise. "So I get to wear this."

Then she ripped the fedora off Daddy Sparky's head.

* * * * * * * *

At Kids' Castle, Annie pulled the Hummer around back so no one would observe her dive into the back seat wearing her Daddy disguise and then emerge in a frilly dress—she'd even stuck a bow in her short hair!

"You'll make everyone suspicious," Rebecca scoffed. "With that bow in your hair, you don't even look like you!"

But Annie ignored her. It took Jackie, Marcia, Petal, and Zinnia all working together to carry in the huge present we had gotten for Will.

"Annie, Durinda, Georgia, Jackie, Marcia, Petal, Rebecca, Zinnia—how good of you all to come!" Mrs. Simms said.

We really liked Will's mother. She always got our names right.

"My, how pretty you all look!" Mrs. Simms went on. "I have trouble dressing one boy, but look at the job your mother does with eight."

Annie scowled at this. Our appearance that day had nothing to do with our mother and everything to do with her.

"And what an enormous birthday present!" Mrs. Simms clapped. "I'm sure Will will love it, whatever it is. But where are your parents?"

All around Kids' Castle, there were parents. Parents, parents everywhere, and not a single pair were ours. It was enough to drive a person to drink juice boxes.

"They just had, er, some errands to run," Annie said. "Don't worry."

Will was playing with Mandy Stenko on the jungle bars, but when he saw us, he came over. He had on dressy clothes, his hair slicked back.

"I'm really glad you all could make it." Will looked relieved. Who could blame him? Without us, he'd have been stuck with just Mandy.

"We wouldn't miss it for the world," Zinnia said.

"So, you're nine now." Rebecca punched Will lightly on the shoulder.

Will rubbed his arm. Apparently, the punch hadn't been that light.

"Don't worry," Will said amiably, "you'll get there too. I mean, if you just keep getting older, it's bound to happen, right?"

Mrs. Simms showed us where to put our present, which we had wrapped as well as we could. We placed it next to the only other present.

"Who wrapped your present," Mandy Stenko shouted to us from where she was swinging upside down on the jungle bars, "your cats?"

It was, sadly, true: our present did look ratty—at

least the wrapping paper did—when placed beside Mandy's perfectly wrapped one.

"*Our* mother," Annie replied with the testiness of a Georgia or a Rebecca, "was too busy coming up with inventions to save the world to bother with something as silly as wrapping a present perfectly, especially when Will's only going to rip the paper off."

Will rescued the moment by inviting us to join in the play.

But that wasn't as much fun as it normally would have been, because Annie kept yelling at us not to hang upside down or do tumbling.

"But we have tights on!" Georgia objected.

"Doesn't matter," Annie said.

This really was too much. For although Mommy would have made us wear dresses to a party, she never would have stopped us from hanging.

"A woman," Mommy always said, "should always look like a lady. *But,*" she would add, "a scientist should never let fashion get in the way."

Even if Annie was sometimes good at being Daddy, she was definitely no Mommy. So we mostly sat on our hands in chairs as Mandy had all the fun with Will. Mandy's mother had let *her* wear jeans and a T-shirt to the party, and as Rebecca put it, she looked like a mechanic.

When it was time for pizza, at least we had something to do. But Annie insisted we use utensils so we wouldn't drip on our dresses.

Our absent Mommy had been given credit by Mrs. Simms for our pretty clothes. Our absent Mommy had been accused by Mandy of being a poor present wrapper. And everywhere we looked, there were still parents milling. It made Annie try all the harder to be our parent.

Cake time was better, because everyone else had to eat with a fork also. We silently thanked the universe that it was a sheet cake. If it had been cupcakes, Annie probably would have made us use utensils for those too.

"I must say," Rebecca muttered to Annie as she ate the frosting, "you're not making this fun. We might as well be at home cleaning toilets."

It was unfortunate she said that, because Annie had yet to assign any of us to toilet-cleaning detail, and even the cats had started to complain.

But then it was present-opening time. If you can't have your own presents it is almost as much fun watching someone else open up his.

Moving from smallest to largest, Will opened Mandy Stenko's first.

"Wow," he said flatly, trying to muster enthusiasm, "a soccer ball."

"Will hates soccer," Rebecca said.

"No, he doesn't," Mandy hissed. "Didn't you all see how enthusiastic he was when Mrs. McGillicuddy gave him those trading cards? And *you*," she accused Jackie, "you said it was the wave of the future."

"Did I?" Jackie said. "I *meant* to say it's a silly game. The only reason anyone ever plays it is if they have no imagination."

"Why do you all always have to be so mean?" Mandy asked.

"We're not," Jackie said. "We just don't see why you can never pay attention to people. If you paid attention to Will—outside of us, he *is* your only classmate—you'd know he hates soccer. Everyone knows, except for you and the McG." She turned to Mrs. Simms. "Isn't that right?"

We didn't think Mrs. Simms liked to hurt any child's feelings, but: "He hates it," she said at last, "even worse than taking medicine."

"We're sorry, Mandy," Jackie said, "we wish it weren't true, but it is."

Mandy scowled.

To break the mood, Will opened our present.

"Oh. *My.*" It was all Mrs. Simms could say at the grandiosity of it.

"I've always wanted one of these!" Will practically

shouted. "Well, I didn't actually know they even made anything like this. But I always dreamed that someday someone might invent it and I knew I'd want one." He turned to his mother. "Can we set it up right here?"

"Oh, Will," that nice lady said sadly, "I don't think the Kids' Castle people would like that. Besides"—she consulted her watch—"it's just about time for the party to end. Mandy's mother is already here"—of course Mandy Stenko's mother was there; it seemed like everyone in the whole *world's* parents were already there—"so we just need to wait for the girls' parents to arrive and then it'll be time for us to go too."

The girls' parents. Hmm . . . where were they?

CHAPTER NINE

We waited, the clock ticking more loudly minute by minute.

"Hmm," Jackie said, "I wonder what's keeping Daddy?"

"You know," Marcia said to Mrs. Simms, "you really can go now. We can wait for Daddy by ourselves. I'm sure he'll be along any moment."

"Don't be ridiculous," Mrs. Simms said. "What kind of hostess would I be? Besides, it's probably against the law."

"Excuse me," Annie said abruptly. "I need to go to the bathroom."

Then Rebecca created a diversion by asking if she could have some more frosting—"please!"—so Mrs. Simms didn't notice that rather than head for the bathroom, Annie raced straight for the back door.

Five minutes later, enough time for Rebecca to get

frosting all over her frock, we heard the sound of a horn honking. Loudly.

It was the Hummer.

"Ooh, that must be Daddy!" Jackie said as we all put on our coats, not even bothering to peek in the goody bags Mrs. Simms handed us.

"Well, goodbye!" Zinnia piped up. "Happy birthday again!"

Mrs. Simms squinted out the back door. "Has your father grown a mustache since I last saw him?"

"Oh, yes," Jackie said. "You know . . . *France.*"

"I should at least say hello to him." Mrs. Simms started for the door.

"Oh, no!" Jackie said. "I mean, didn't Will say his family party is tonight? I suspect you'd want to hurry. And you still have packages to bring out to your car, you know, *out front.* We'd hate to keep you, so . . ."

"Goodbye again!" Zinnia said.

We rushed out before Mrs. Simms could say anything else. Then we buckled ourselves in and waited for her to totally and completely leave, meaning the parking lot as well. Because of course she was parked in front, like any normal person would be, while we were in the back.

"Some party that was for us, thanks to you," Rebecca said to Annie. "It was about as much fun as the one on New Year's Eve."

"Okay." Annie ignored Rebecca and put the key in the ignition. "Everybody ready?"

We said that we were, but when she turned the key, nothing happened.

"Are you putting your hand on the gas hard enough?" Annie called to Durinda, down beneath her legs.

"Of course I am!" Durinda said, annoyed. "You know, eventually we're going to have to devise a more efficient way of doing this. This can't be safe for everyone else, and it's certainly not safe for me."

"Well, press harder," Annie instructed.

But however hard Durinda pressed, and her grunts told us she was pressing very hard, it wasn't hard enough.

"What are we going to do?" Georgia asked.

"It's too far to walk." Petal's lip quivered. "We'll freeze to death."

"There's nothing for it." Annie picked up the car phone, a device none of us had ever used before. "I'll just have to call Pete." She went through her usual routine—call Information, wait, impersonate Daddy, beg Pete to come help out for double the pay, call him "old chap," and ring off—after which she quickly changed back into her party clothes.

"You look ridiculous," Rebecca said. "Have I mentioned that before?"

"Pretty much," Annie said, "but we can't have Pete seeing me in my Daddy-driving-the-car disguise. He'll know something is up then."

"Like he won't already." Rebecca snickered.

"That's not helpful," Annie said, then as the snow started to fall gently, we all waited in silence for Pete to come.

When he got there, we were hugely relieved. Kids' Castle had closed for the day, and soon it would be dark.

"Hullo, Eights," he said as we all got out to greet him. "What seems to be the problem with the Hummer? And where, by the way, is your dad?"

"In the bathroom," Jackie said.

"Gone for coffee," Marcia said at the same time.

"Huh," Pete said. "And here I thought you'd say he was in France."

"That's Mommy," Zinnia said earnestly. "Weren't you paying proper attention that time you came to visit us?"

"Right-o," Pete said. "Well, while we're waiting for your dad to reappear from . . . *wherever he is,* why don't I look at the car for you?"

Which is what he did, moving to climb behind the wheel, but first . . .

"Huh," he said, the falling snow making his hair

look like he had more salt than pepper in it now. "Has your dad shrunk since I last saw him? I don't remember him needing to sit on dictionaries to drive his own car."

"They're reference materials," Jackie said. "Mommy's." Then she finished lamely, having run out of lies, "I don't know how they got there."

"Never mind," Pete said, moving them out of the way. "But you must admit, it is all very strange: dictionaries appearing where they shouldn't be, your dad suddenly speaking with a British accent . . ."

"Is there any reason why he couldn't be British?" Annie asked irritably. She was sensitive about her Daddy accent. "Couldn't we *all* be British?"

"Sure," Pete said agreeably enough as he moved the seat back, "why not? I mean, we do all *sound* sort of British when we talk. For all we know, we *are* in England." He turned the key in the ignition, but nothing happened.

"Huh," Pete said. "I was sure you were calling me out here on another false alarm, but there really is something wrong." He popped the hood, got out, and started rooting around where we thought the engine might be.

A minute passed, two, three, the sky getting darker all the while. At last we heard a low whistle. Pete's head popped up, and then his hand. In it was a long piece of black rubber with copper wires sticking out of it.

"What's that?" Annie asked. "Did the driver somehow, er, break it?"

"By *driver* you mean your dad?" Pete asked. When Annie nodded, he went on. "No. I'm afraid this is a case of . . . sabotage." He eyed us all. "First, you have me come out to the house when nothing is wrong with your car, and now you have me come out here only to find a car that's been tampered with." His gaze narrowed. "Are you sure one of you doesn't have a crush on me and is trying to capture my attention?"

"God, *no!*" we all said at once.

"Do you honestly think," Annie said, raising herself up with the pride of an adult, "that any one of us would *do* something like that?"

Pete studied us for a long time.

"No," he finally admitted. "I suppose not. But then . . ."

"Then *what?*" Annie said.

"Then if it wasn't any of you, someone—*some other person*—did this. Someone wanted to make sure you wouldn't get home. Or at the very least, that you'd be delayed. Do you have any idea who?"

"No!" we all said. But now we were worried. We had to get home.

"Please, Mr. Pete," Annie begged on our behalf, "is there anything you can do to fix the car?"

"Of course," he said. He got cables and did some stuff. Then he got back behind the wheel and tried the starter again. This time, it hummed.

"We don't know how to thank you," Annie said. "I mean, with a check, of course. But, er, Daddy left the house today without his checkbook . . ."

"No worries," Pete said. "I've always trusted your dad. But . . . my, my, my, he has been gone at the coffee-bathroom for a long time." He paused. "And I really wouldn't feel right leaving until he returns."

Blasted adults! The ones you wanted disappeared on New Year's Eve and the rest kept sticking their nose in your business.

"Please, Mr. Pete." Now Annie was begging in a way we'd never seen her do before; there were practically tears in her eyes. "Please don't wait for our father to return. He can't come back to drive the car if you're here. So if you do wait, you might be waiting for—"

We were all sure she was about to say *forever,* but she never got the chance because Pete, perhaps feeling sorry for her, cut her off.

"Stop babbling, lamb," he said gently. "If it makes you fret so to have me wait, I won't do it. But do me just one favor, to ease my mind."

"Anything," Annie promised. "Anything!"

Pete disappeared inside his van again, then returned with two large wooden blocks to which he'd attached giant rubber bands.

"Here," he offered, holding them out to Annie, "I have the feeling your dad has grown shorter since I last saw him. If he puts these on the gas and brake, he should have no trouble reaching them."

Now there really were tears in Annie's eyes.

"Thanks," she said, rising up on tippytoes to lay a kiss on Pete's stubbly cheek. "You're the best mechanic *ever!*"

"Thank you." Pete touched the place where he'd been kissed. "Almost no one ever kisses me." Then he got serious again as he moved toward his truck, calling, "And promise me one more thing?"

"Anything," Annie said again. "Anything!"

"You still have my number?" he asked.

We nodded.

"Promise me you'll use it if you ever need someone to help you with emergencies even bigger than cars that are perfectly fine or cars that won't start. I'm going to be worrying about you lot."

"You don't need to worry about us, Mr. Pete," Annie said. "We're the Sisters Eight, after all. But I promise, if we need you, we'll call."

* * * * * * * *

The ride home was less hair-raising than the previous rides had been, even with the falling snow. With those new blocks on the pedals, Annie could now drive without help.

But it was still hair-raising because we didn't know what we were going home to. Someone had cut a cable in our car, delaying our arrival home. Someone maybe didn't want us to get home at all.

And yet, although we were filled with fear and anticipation, we were tired too.

"It is exhausting," Jackie said, "telling all of these lies to people. Do you think it's wrong of us to do it? Do you think it makes us bad people?"

"No," Annie said slowly, as though she were working the thoughts out even as she was speaking the words, "I don't. Adults train us to tell white lies all the time. They say, 'Tell Aunt Martha she doesn't look fat in that dress.' They say, 'Tell Uncle George his cooking tastes great.' None of that stuff is ever true, but we have to say it to save other people's feelings. Well, now we have to save something bigger: we have to save Mommy and Daddy, maybe even ourselves. If we can lie about fat clothes and bad food and it's okay, I don't see anything wrong with lying to save people's lives. Even if we are having fun while we're doing so."

We were silent for a long moment, digesting all that she had said. Annie really had grown as smart as any adult we knew. Then:

"What do you think is going on at our house right now?" Georgia asked.

"To that," Annie said, driving on into the night, "I have no answer."

CHAPTER TEN

Annie parked the Hummer at the bottom of the drive and killed the lights.

"What are you doing?" Rebecca asked.

"I'm creating the element of surprise," Annie said. "If someone is in the house, it would be better if they didn't see us coming."

"Shouldn't we run the other way?" Petal said.

"No," Annie said. "There are eight of us. Whoever might be up there can't catch all of us at once. We could probably overpower whoever it is. Or at the very least, some of us would be able to get away to tell the tale."

"You don't make that sound very encouraging," Georgia said. "Maybe we'd be better off calling the police?"

"Or maybe we could smoke the person out with a fire?" Rebecca suggested.

"I keep telling you," Annie said, ignoring Rebecca,

"the police can't help people like us. They're equipped to handle kids getting kidnapped but not parents getting parentnapped."

"What about Pete?" Georgia pressed. "He comes when we call."

"True," Annie said. Then we saw her shrug in the dark of the car. "But he knows now that we're on our own. If we call him, he'll rethink leaving us that way and turn us in to the coppers."

"What are we going to do, then?" Marcia asked.

"We're going home," Annie said simply.

Then she got out of the car, inviting all of us to do the same.

"I'm not dressed for walking up the driveway in new snow," Petal said.

"I don't like to complain," Zinnia added, "but I am sliding around."

"Hold on to each other's hands," Annie advised, starting a chain. "If we hold on to each other, we'll hold each other up."

"Or," Rebecca said, "one of us will fall, bringing the rest down with her, like dominoes." But she took hold of Georgia's hand just the same and now our chain of eight stretched across the whole driveway.

"We're like a line of linebackers," Marcia said with a nervous giggle.

"Or a line of cut-out paper dolls," Zinnia said.

"Or a line of idiots," Rebecca said.

"Shh," Annie whispered. "We're getting closer."

Now that we were practically upon the house, we sensed that something was wrong.

"There are no lights on," Marcia observed. "If it wasn't for the moonlight, we wouldn't be able to see anything. It's too dark."

"Of course it's dark," Annie hissed. "We didn't leave any lights on."

"But why didn't we?" Jackie asked. "What are we, nuts?"

"We may be," Annie said, "but that's not it. We didn't leave any lights on because we thought we'd be coming home in daylight. We didn't plan on someone sabotaging the Hummer."

"So what will we do when we go in?" Marcia asked. "Will we leave the lights off in case the intruder, if there is one, is still there?"

"Maybe we could bark like a pack of mean dogs to scare the intruder off," Rebecca suggested.

"Don't be daft," Annie said, ignoring Rebecca. "How will we find anything in the dark? Besides, if we leave it dark, someone could sneak up behind us."

We were on the stoop now and we waited, scared, as Annie slowly turned the doorknob. As she turned it, we heard a flutter. In the moonlight, we saw a carrier pigeon, perhaps the one who'd visited us before, circle the house and then fly away.

"I wonder what he wanted," Durinda said, watching him go.

"I guess we'll never know," Annie said. Then she opened the door.

The moonlight revealed a delegation of eight cats waiting for us right inside the door. This was not unusual. We'd been gone longer than planned, and they were probably hungry. Either that or they were planning to lodge another complaint about the condition of the human toilets.

"Meow!" Anthrax said as soon as we were in the door.

"Yes, I know you're hungry," Annie whispered, "and we'll feed you as soon as we can, but we need to take care of something else first."

"Meow!" Anthrax said more violently as Annie switched on the lights.

"Really," Annie started to say, "I promise we'll—"

But Zinnia cut her off. "She's not complaining about hunger," she said. "She's trying to tell us something else."

"How would you know?" Rebecca scoffed. "I suppose you think the cats are talking to you again?"

But Annie ignored Rebecca's scoffing of Zinnia, even if Zinnia didn't.

"Let's look around," Annie said. "We need to investigate each room."

"Shall I run ahead and get your spear for you?" Georgia offered.

We'd noticed that Georgia had changed somewhat. She could still be as testy as Rebecca, but it was as though seeing Annie take charge of the household had caused a grudging admiration to grow in her.

"No, thank you," Annie said. "If you run ahead without us, you might get yourself killed."

That shut Georgia up. That shut all of us up. We were that scared.

The front room was the obvious first room to investigate because, well, it was right there.

"Daddy and Mommy are missing!" Marcia observed with a cry.

"Of course they're missing," Georgia said, proving that while she might now admire Annie, she didn't necessarily admire the rest of us. "They've been missing for weeks!"

"Or dead," Rebecca added.

"I don't mean that," Marcia said. "I mean Daddy Sparky and Mommy Sally." She indicated the spot near the window where they had spent most of their time.

"They're not there."

"That's because we moved them to the drawing room so they could have tea while we were at Will's party," Georgia said. "Don't you remember?"

"Oh, right," Marcia said.

It was obvious at a glance that nothing had been disturbed.

But something was still wrong.

The cats were going crazy.

As we tried to move through the front room to the rooms beyond, they kept circling our feet and tripping us up.

"What is the *matter* with all of you?" Annie said, in her annoyance speaking louder than she had been. "Now look what you've done! You've made me speak too loudly, as a result of which the jig is probably up!"

Anthrax would normally have been cowed by the tone in Annie's voice. But instead, she continued to *meow!* loudly, as though she really were trying to tell us something.

"What is it?" Annie hissed.

Anthrax tilted her head upward, making a great show of inhaling. She kept doing it, flaring her nostrils each time.

"I really do think she is trying to tell us something," Zinnia offered.

"Yes, but what?" Annie said.

"I think she wants us to try doing what she's doing," Zinnia said, tilting her own head upward. "Maybe then we'll find out."

Feeling ridiculous, we all did what Anthrax and Zinnia were doing. At first, we smelled nothing. Perhaps the long walk up the driveway had interfered with our sense of smell. Could our nostrils be frozen?

But then, there it was: the faint odor of . . . what was that?

"Fruitcake," Annie said with certainty. "I smell fruit-cake."

"Are you quite sure?" Marcia asked. "But that's not possible. You threw out the fruitcake the Wicket brought us right after she left that night. The odor should be long gone." She turned to Durinda. "Haven't you taken out the trash since then?"

"Of course," Durinda said. "What kind of slob do you take me for?"

Annie, with Anthrax at her side, led us toward the kitchen, our noses sniffing the air all the while.

But when we got there, it was like playing the game Too Hot, Too Cold, and the scent was almost nonexistent.

"Let's try the other rooms," Annie suggested.

And so we moved on, noses in the air, turning on lights as we went.

We checked the drawing room, cautiously peeking our heads around the corner, one head topping the next from shortest to tallest. We were relieved to find Daddy Sparky and Mommy Sally still having tea. The scent seemed slightly stronger than in the front room, but we looked around and couldn't see anything that had been disturbed.

"Check behind the loose stone to see if another note or something has been left there," Jackie suggested.

But when we looked, there was only empty darkness.

Next we tried Daddy's study, with similar results: a stronger scent than the front room, but no disturbances.

We checked Winter, Spring, Summer, Fall. There was nothing except for in Summer, where the cats had apparently used the beach sand there as a litter box, in a sign of protest.

"Let's check upstairs next," Annie said.

"But shouldn't we first—" Jackie started, but Annie cut her off.

"No," Annie said. "We'll leave *that* room"—and we all knew which room she was talking about—"for last."

But upstairs, the scent was dead cold: no fruitcake aroma at all. Not to mention the cats were going crazy again. They kept circling us, jerking their little heads toward the hallway and the stairs. They were looking at us like we were crazy. Or stupid.

"I guess there really is no avoiding it any longer," Annie said, and we followed once again as she and Anthrax led us all back downstairs.

Once we were at the bottom, Annie placed her hand on Georgia's arm and in a tone of total seriousness said, "Please get the spear now."

Which Georgia did, looking very grim.

With Annie armed ahead of us, we at last approached the closed door to . . . Mommy's study.

It was the one room in the house our parents had never allowed us to roam through freely. And since they'd disappeared—or died—other than briefly checking it on New Year's Eve, we'd avoided it like, well, the plague, or at the very least a nest of hornets. Even though our parents were gone, we couldn't disobey their strictest orders. We might eat pink frosting straight from the can or drive their car, but we wouldn't go in Mommy's private study.

But now we had to. There was no other choice.

The smell there was the strongest it'd been yet. More, there was a cold draft coming from beneath the closed door.

"It hasn't been cold like this back here before," Durinda said. "I'm sure I'd have noticed that when I vacuumed the hallways."

"This is no time to defend your cleaning practices,"

Annie whispered, and she slowly turned the knob on Mommy's study door.

But as she pushed the door open, some force on the other side shoved it closed.

Annie turned the knob again, pressed back against the door with all her might, and wedged the door open a half inch.

The force on the other side pressed harder, and it slammed it shut.

Not even thinking of the danger, we threw our bodies against the closed door, helping Annie push. All we knew was we needed to get in.

This time, we succeeded in pushing the door open a full inch.

But the force on the other side must have been very strong, for the door then slammed shut, and we heard the click of a lock.

"Quick! Get the key!" Annie commanded to someone, anyone.

Jackie raced off and quickly returned with the key.

The key turned with ease, and this time the door gave easily as we pressed against it.

The smell hit us as soon as the door was opened, a smell of fruitcake so big and awful, we gagged.

Worse, the light on Mommy's desk was on and the window behind the desk was wide open. The wind made

the sheer white curtains dance into the room.

We all tried to settle our racing hearts and not think that just a short time ago a stranger, possibly a dangerous stranger, had been in our home, in this very room.

It had been so long since anyone had been in there, a fine layer of dust covered everything. There were even cobwebs in the corners. But the purple walls still looked pretty.

"I'll need to get a ladder to see to those," Durinda said of the cobwebs.

"Never mind that now," Annie said.

"But, um," Petal said, "aren't we in danger?"

"I don't think so," Annie said, "at least not at the moment. Whoever was in here must have escaped by that window."

"But they could come back at any time," Jackie said

sensibly, "and then we'd be in danger again."

"True," Annie admitted, "but they're not here right now. The danger has passed for the time being. Look: even the cats are calm again."

It was true. Despite the overwhelming smell of fruitcake in the air, the cats looked peaceful now, all but Anthrax settling themselves in for a nice nap in various spots around the room.

"What's this?" Annie said. She had moved to the other side of Mommy's desk to close the window. She bent down and picked up a manila envelope from the floor.

She showed us the front. In big red block letters that almost screamed, it said TOP SECRET.

Annie opened it, spreading the leaves outward, but nothing fell out.

It was empty.

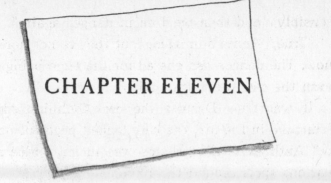

CHAPTER ELEVEN

"I can't believe this," Annie said, awe in her voice.

"What?" Jackie asked.

"I told the Wicket that Mommy was working on something top secret . . . and there really is a Top Secret folder!"

"What does it mean?" Marcia said.

"Who cares about some stupid folder?" Rebecca said. "Someone's been in our home, and they left this wretched fruitcake smell!"

"I care about some stupid folder," Annie said. She propped her spear against the wall, then lowered herself into the black leather seat behind Mommy's desk. "As should we all."

"But why?" Rebecca countered. "It doesn't mean anything. It's just—"

"Of course it means something," Annie said.

"*Everything* means *something,* even when that something isn't important. *Think.*"

So we all thought, the only sound in the room the sound of cats purring in their sleep. Loudly.

"Who's the only person we know," Annie said, "that makes fruitcakes?"

"*The Wicket!*" Jackie said, the gleam of knowledge entering her eye.

"Exactly," Annie said. "Too bad I made my smooth move of lying about Mommy working on something top secret in front of the wrong person."

"How do you mean?" Marcia asked.

"Think back to that night," Annie said. "Think back to how interested the Wicket got when I said Mommy was working on something."

It was true.

"And," Annie went on, "what sort of person asks questions about the work of a scientist? That's never happened to us before. Everyone asks questions about Daddy's being a model. They think it must be glamorous, I suppose. But *no one* asks questions about Mommy's work."

That was true too. And who makes fruitcakes anyway?

"This is the way I figure it." Annie paused, causing us to lean forward.

"Yes?" we prompted.

"The way I figure it, the Wicket's always been curious about Mommy's work, only we never noticed. But as soon as I said 'top secret,' she waited for an opportunity. She must have followed us, tampering with our car so we wouldn't surprise her as she tossed Mommy's study." A light dawned in Annie's eyes. "She must know we're alone!"

"But couldn't she have come when we were at school?" Marcia asked.

"You'd think so," Annie said. "But even bad people can be scared. Who knows how criminal minds think?"

We certainly didn't. But we realized we were going to have to learn.

"Maybe she wanted to kill us in our sleep!" Petal said.

"But what did the Wicket want so desperately that she was willing to go to such lengths?" Jackie asked, ignoring Petal. "What could Mommy have been working on that was so important?"

"That's the thing." Annie lifted the Top Secret folder once more, opening it again to reveal its emptiness. "Whatever it is, it's gone now."

"It may be a mystery," Georgia said, "but it doesn't have to be."

"How do you mean?" Annie asked.

There was real fire in Georgia's eyes. She went behind the desk and grabbed the spear from where Annie had propped it against the wall.

"I say," Georgia said, "we go over to the Wicket's right now and *demand* she tell us what's going on. We can be like the thumbscrew boys. We'll torture her if we have to."

"I'm afraid we can't do that," Annie said sadly, then she patted Georgia's arm and gently removed the spear from her grip. "Although I do appreciate the gesture."

"But why can't we?" Georgia countered. "There are eight of us and only one of her. Plus, she's barely as tall as we are. We can take her."

"Or we could just blow up her house!" Rebecca suggested.

"It's not a matter of size," Annie said, ignoring Rebecca. She tapped the side of her head. "It's a matter of brains. We need to be smarter than she is. She's probably expecting us. So we need to bide our time, like she did."

"But why?" Durinda asked. "Even I don't understand the idea behind waiting. I'm with Georgia on this. I say we go over there and smash her."

"What good would that do? And how would we be better off? She'd know we were on to her and we'd be no wiser. No, there was something she came here for tonight. We need to wait until *she's* out of the house and then search *her* place."

"Wow," Georgia said earnestly, "it must take all kinds of energy to be inside your brain right now."

Annie smiled, for the first time in hours, it seemed. "Thank you," she said. The smile disappeared. "But it is exhausting, thinking this much."

We all thought about that for a moment, about what it must be like to be Annie right now.

Then, into the sound of the silence made by our thinking, we heard someone crying. We looked around at the usual suspects.

Petal? No.

Zinnia? No.

It wasn't any of the people we thought it might be. It was Rebecca.

"What's wrong?" Annie asked gently.

"This!" Rebecca gestured wildly with her arms, the tears streaking her cheeks. "All of *this!*"

"What *this* do you mean?" Annie asked.

"Maybe," Rebecca said, wiping at her eyes fiercely, "you should be asking what *isn't* wrong, since nearly everything is."

"I still don't understand," Annie said, "but I'm trying to."

"It's just that . . . it's just that . . . it's just that

tonight makes everything seem so final!" Rebecca burst out. "Before"—she brushed fresh tears from her cheek with a sleeve—"I could tell myself that Mommy and Daddy disappeared into some magical place, but that they'd be coming back any minute now. It was just a matter of waiting. Nothing awful had happened, not really. It was just a game."

"But we all thought you were glad Mommy and Daddy were gone," Jackie said. "In fact, we thought you wanted them gone forever."

"No." Rebecca shook her head. "I only wanted them to be gone for a little while. I wanted them to be gone long enough for me to eat a can of pink frosting and slide down the banister and swing from the chandelier. But I never wanted them to be gone *forever*." She paused. "But all of this: with our house getting broken into and the Wicket smelling like fruitcake and that empty Top Secret folder. It's all too real now. Mommy and Daddy didn't disappear on a lark. They disappeared for a reason. And—"

"Shh, shh." Annie soothed her, stopping Rebecca's words as she took her in her arms. "It's still a game," she said. "We just haven't quite figured out how to play it yet."

Then Durinda made us all cocoa while Annie and Georgia moved around the house, making sure all the doors and windows were locked.

Even robot Betty seemed to feel sorry for us now. When Durinda asked her to clean off the kitchen table, she actually did it properly.

"I yelled at Daddy Sparky and Mommy Sally," Annie said, at last taking her seat at the head of the table. "Fine pair of watchdogs they are."

"It's not really their fault though, is it?" Zinnia said. Then she yawned, setting off a round of yawning among us. We were all so tired. It had been a long day.

"The refrigerator said this is the last of the milk," Durinda said with a sigh, taking a sip of her cocoa. It was good cocoa, with mini marshmallows floating on the top. "So what's our next move?" she asked Annie.

"I'm not sure," Annie admitted. "But this all started with that note on New Year's Eve. The note said we each had to find our power and our gift. I've got the first, but I still don't have the second." She yawned. "And none of you have your powers or gifts yet."

We sipped some more cocoa.

"So what's next?" Durinda asked again.

"Bed," Annie said. "Bed."

CHAPTER TWELVE

We bided our time, as Annie had instructed, but as we moved through the closing days of January, there was no opportunity to act.

The Wicket never left the house anymore, even though a thaw had come; the snow was melting so quickly, small rivers were running down the sides of the streets, and the icicles that had previously hung from the rooftops had long since drip-dripped away. We watched the Wicket's front door through binoculars, but she was even having her food delivered. There was no chance to investigate. Nor were there any gifts in sight.

Finally, on the last day of January, Annie had had enough.

"I *have* to find my gift today!" she said. "I just *have* to!"

"Why today?" Rebecca asked. "Is there some special reason?"

"I don't know," Annie said. "But I have this feeling

that if I *don't* find my gift today, my time to do so will have expired!"

"Why not check the loose stone in the drawing room again?" Zinnia said, grabbing an apple from the bowl on the table. Annie's insistence that we all eat five fruits and veggies a day was finally starting to rub off on us.

"Well, that's the most ridiculous idea I've ever heard," Annie said. "We check there every morning, but there's never anything there."

"But Zither swore she saw that loose stone move while we were out," Zinnia insisted. "All the cats are talking about it."

We rolled our eyes. Talking cats! What would this kid think of next?

"Fine. Then I'll check." Zinnia shrugged, chomping her apple as she left the kitchen.

A moment later, we heard: "Annie! Come quick!"

We raced to the drawing room, where Zinnia was standing in front of the rectangular hole. She'd removed the loose stone, and whatever she saw must have shocked her, because she'd stopped chomping her apple.

"What is it?" Annie asked, looking almost scared.

"I think I see something glittering in there," Zinnia said. "But I'm too scared to touch it. What if it's magic? *Bad* magic?" Then: "Hey, do you think it might be for me? Maybe it's my gift. After all, I found it."

"Don't touch it!" Georgia shouted at Zinnia. Then she nodded her head at Annie. "Go ahead," she said. "I'm sure it will be all right."

Annie moved forward to see what was in the darkness of the hole, still looking scared. Slowly, she put her hand inside, and when her hand came back out, she was holding a ring. It was a beautiful ring, the stone large and diamond shaped, in an old-fashioned gold setting. The stone in the ring was purple, our mother's favorite color.

"Put it on," Jackie urged.

Annie did so. Even though the ring had looked big enough to fit an adult, when Annie tried it on, it fit perfectly.

"Oh," Zinnia said, her face falling. "It must be your gift and not mine, after all. My fingers"—she held one hand out sadly—"are much too small to wear something like that."

"You'll find your gift," Annie said soothingly. "Everyone will. I'm sure of it."

"But do you think it can possibly work that way?" Jackie asked. "One of us finding the gift for another of us, like Zinnia did for you, Annie?"

Annie shrugged. "I don't see why it couldn't." She thought about it for a moment. "I think we each have to find our powers on our own. But our gifts?" She shrugged again. "I suppose there's no reason we can't help each other with those."

"But how do you know all that?" Rebecca asked.

"I don't know." Annie shrugged one last time. "I just feel like I do."

Annie moved to put the loose stone back in place, and her eyes lit on something else.

"Hey!" she said. "There's another note in here!"

"Read it! Read it!" we all urged.

Dear Annie,

Congratulations on finding the gift that goes along with your power. I'm sure someone, somewhere, is very proud of you. Now your seven sisters need to get busy finding their gifts and powers. They can take their time . . . but not too long! Two down, fourteen to go . . .

"Huh," Durinda said, sounding a little bit like Pete. "This note seems almost friendly. I wonder who's leaving them?"

"Or *what's* leaving them," Rebecca added darkly.

"Do you ever get the strange feeling that someone is telling our story?" Marcia wondered aloud.

"I do," Jackie said. "And then I always wonder if that same person isn't leaving these notes."

"So," Georgia said to Annie, "now that you have your power and your gift, do you have a new plan for us yet?"

"I do," Annie said, fingering her ring, "sort of. We go on searching for our powers and our gifts and, in the meantime, we try to discover what Mommy was working on, what was in that Top Secret file when she and Daddy disappeared. I have the feeling that whoever or whatever is behind all of this, the answer lies there."

She took a deep breath, then spoke again.

"I think," she said, "our adventures are only just beginning."